SALVADOR

SOUTH MAFIA WARS

PAIGE PRICE

IG Publishing Partners, LLC

From author Paige Price comes a mafia strangers-to-lovers romance about a mafia soldier and the girl who captures his heart . . .

Heroes come in all shapes, sizes, and personalities.

Mine is tall, ripped, silent, and a strategist, not to mention deadly.

He's not the man I thought he was. No, Salvador Vargas is so much more.

Ardent

Principled

Level-Headed

The man chooses honor and loyalty over materialistic things or power at every turn.

During a barroom brawl, he comes to my aid without a hint of hesitation.

I should've thanked him, then went on about my day, my life.

Cindy Stevens hides behind a plastic façade, never showing the scars of her pain.
But in a moment of weakness, she lets down her guard, allowing me inside.

Scarred
  Damaged
  Beautifully Flawed

She's a pawn in her father's game of chess, one he seeks to control and dominate for power.
The more she pulls away from him, the tighter the top-notch attorney tightens the noose.
She yearns for freedom, to break free of his paternal hold and escape her gilded cage.

The girl beneath the plastic mask holds my heart.
One look.
One secret touch.
One blissfully hot kiss.
And we're both falling and fast.

In my world, she is the forbidden fruit—a fruit I desperately yearn to devour.

It's wrong to claim her as mine, but it doesn't matter because the girl, she's mine!

SOUTH MAFIA WARS

Dominic

Augustin

Juan Carlos

Salvador

Clemente

Trenton

Joaquin

Yasmina

You can find the "Series Page" HERE!

Want more South Mafia Wars?

Sign up for the newsletter HERE!

South MAFIA WARS

SALVADOR
South Mafia Wars
COPYRIGHT©2022
Paige Price
Cover Design by Wren Taylor

Published in the United States of America by:

DLG Publishing Partners
PO Box 17674
San Antonio, TX 78217
www.DLGPublishingPartners.com

For all those 'bad boy' boyfriends!

AUTHOR'S NOTE

To my readers,

Thank you for taking a chance on me and reading my books. It means the world to me.

Subscribe to my newsletter to get updates about upcoming books:

www.subscribepage.com/southmafiawars

CONTENTS

MINE TO HOLD

Cindy Stevens

"Please, have a seat, gentlemen." Playing hostess to an ex-boyfriend who refused to stay in the friend zone didn't bode well. And it didn't help that Keegan Black's besties, Kyle Lubbock, Tobin Tilly, and Benjamin Reid, accompanied him like unshakeable shadows. "Ophelia will be over momentarily to take your drink orders."

Somehow, I had managed to smile anyway, and not one of those go-to-hell forced ones either. An actual one because my grandmother always said that a warm, sincere smile was the universal language of kindness and compassion. Plus, I read somewhere that it takes like forty-three muscles to frown and only seventeen to smile. Not to mention, smiling—a real bona fide one—led to physiological changes in the brain that cooled the blood and, in turn, made a person feel happier.

And right now, I need all the sunshine and happiness a girl can get.

Ophelia Maldonado's head bobbed, then her tempestuous gaze latched onto mine.

The woman had made it her mission in life to make me feel less than welcome. And with her openly outward hatred, I often wondered what had happened to leave her so bristly around the edges. Of course, no "mean girl's" club was complete without elite members—individual roles Katie Moore and Gina Aquino gladly filled and took to heart.

"What?" asked Ophelia Maldonado, a slight Mexican accent coating her word. She offered a sour expression to match her bitter attitude and tart mood.

"I think they're ready to order their drinks." Two quick steps away from Keegan, and his hand wrapped around my wrist, yanking me to him like a Yo-Yo on a string.

"Check it out, ladies." Ophelia's gaze flicked from Katie to Gina. "Malibu fuckin' Barbie thinks she's in charge."

God, not now. Why can't she just cut me a break for once?

An ardent sigh left my lips, and I turned my attention to the leech latched onto me.

"Let go. Please." Again, I shot a smile Keegan's way, hoping to deescalate the mounting tension and evolving situation.

Another saying of my grandmother came to mind: *one catches more flies with honey than vinegar.*

But my controlling ex wasn't a pesky fly who tolerated a shooing or a firm swatting.

"That's no way to talk to your fiancé, now, is it?" Keegan's Bostonian accent gave his voice an upward inflection at the end of his sentence.

He dragged me onto his lap.

"Keegan, please. I'm at work." My voice remained calm, but inside, chaos ruled my emotions. "And I'm not your betrothed anymore, remember? We talked about this two weeks ago and agreed that—"

"I didn't agree to shit," he whispered in my ear. "You've had more than enough space, and now it's time to kiss and makeup. Even your father agrees."

"What? No." My bubbly façade slipped a bit. "That's not happening." I shook my head. The ends of my shoulder-length blonde hair whipped my face. "It's over."

"What can I get for ya?" Ophelia approached, unfazed by the scene unfolding.

"A pitcher of beer and six shots." Keegan's fingers dug into my hips, keeping me on his lap. "Make 'em Alabama Slammers." He pressed his erection between my butt cheeks. "We're celebrating."

"Sounds like fun." Ophelia slid her tongue over her cherry red lips.

I'm not celebrating shit with you, I thought, wishing I could scream the words.

But instead of voicing what weighed heavy on my mind, I remained silent.

My body fought to control the emotions threatening to surface, and anger rose the fastest among them.

The fabric of his slacks, as well as my rayon-poly blended pants, did little to conceal his stiff shaft.

"You got it, Darlin'." Ophelia winked, then sashayed away, drawing the eyes of the men at the table, including Keegan's.

"I'd like to fuck that." Kyle chuckled.

"Yeah, I second that." Tobin whistled.

A tirade of voices erupted at the corner of the bar. The source was a group of men—none of them regulars. All Mexicans, if guessing.

What are the chances they're tied to Mina's uncle? The Mad Dog of the South.

It was a thought that left me a bit more unnerved than I already was, which I figured was an impossible feat at this point.

Mina's Russian guy, Dominic, along with the two new Italians, Spider and Marciano, separated some men exchanging blows, then dragged a couple of the men to the door.

God, what I'd give to have someone like that care about me. A sigh left my lips.

"Besides, the firm's annual party's coming up." Keegan pressed his lips to the back of my neck.

My skin crawled as if thousands of tiny ant feet scurried over my flesh.

"Your father will expect the power couple to arrive together," he whispered. "So, it's you and me, babe, just like always."

"People are staring." I tried to keep all traces of anger out of my voice. "And I have work to do."

"Let them stare. I don't care. It's not like it matters." He tightened his grip. "Not anymore, anyway."

"What do you mean?" My heart pounded in my chest, and my palms grew clammy.

"Oh, didn't your dad tell you?"

"Tell me what?" I'd sent my father's calls to voice-mail for the last three days, then deleted them without listening.

Why should I hear what my biological sire has to say, especially when he refuses to listen to my spoken words?

"He gave me his blessing." A grin slithered across his mouth. He continued to hold me in place. "A little help here, Kyle."

"Sure thing." Kyle pulled a black velvety ring box from his pocket, opened it, then extracted a princess-cut engagement ring.

All the air in my body left my lungs in a heavy whoosh of an exhale.

Keegan gripped my left hand, then forced my closed fist open, making me yelp out in pain. He slid the jewelry noose around my ring finger.

"Now that it's official"—Keegan grabbed my hair, then yanked my head back—"You'll do as I say. And I *say* that today is your last day at The Alchemist. Understand."

His lips crashed against mine with brute force. The metallic taste of blood coated my tongue and set my tastebuds off.

"No?" The whispered word left my lips. Once again, I shook my head.

Keegan's eyelids narrowed, and a hint of anger darkened his green eyes.

"Did you just refuse me? Did you say no?" A snarl twisted his mouth.

"Yes. That's what I just said. *No*," I replied. "Hear

me out. You deserve a devoted wife, a loving mother to your future children, and a woman who loves you as much as you love her."

Or as much as you love yourself, you self-centered asshole.

"Keegan, you deserve someone who wants the same things you do. And me, I'm none of those things."

He clenched his teeth, and the muscles of his jaws protruded.

"Don't force my hand," he whispered. "I'll make a scene. You know I will."

Over the years, I'd learned to mask my reactions and keep a light-hearted, happy demeanor because revealing my emotions allowed men like my father, like Keegan, to chip away at my resolve. Hell, at the core of my soul.

I surveyed the room. My gaze landed on a familiar set of coppery brown eyes belonging to Salvador Vargas. His expression, neither judgmental nor amiable, remained detached, like a poker-faced card player.

Once again, Keegan pressed his mouth to mine, but I turned my head. So, his lips grazed the back of my neck.

The contact made me tremble, not out of longing or need, but abhorrence.

Bile rose in the back of my throat. I swallowed hard, then squeezed my lids shut. The sounds of the bar evaporated, leaving me alone with the thumping beat of my heart.

A few seconds ticked by, then my eyes sprung open, only to lock onto Salvador's once again. But this time, unshed tears glistened in my eyes because my father's blessing ended my career as an attorney before it even had a chance to take flight.

A quick yank freed my hand, and I made contact with the side of Keegan's face with an open palm.

The crack of the blow rung in my ears and made my palm sting.

Keegan released me. Once free, I managed to spring from his lap.

"I said, 'No,' Keegan." I pulled the ring from my finger and tossed it at him. "And I meant it. No means no."

"No one talks to me that way." Keegan reached out, and his hand latched onto the sleeve of my shirt. "Especially not you."

He yanked, and the fabric separated at the seam of the shoulder. The motion of the action made me stumble onto the wooden table.

"Seems your girl needs a lesson in manners." Kyle chuckled.

2

Salvador Vargas

"Fuck." The word left my lips in a whisper.

Mina had one main rule when it came to the staff —no one touched them, ever. And by them, I meant the girls. Right now, that fucker, Keegan Black, had his dirty paws all over Cindy.

"What was that?" Andres' voice came across the line, and I gripped the cell at my ear tighter.

"Nothing." I exhaled a calming breath. "Hey, something's come up at the bar. I'll meet you at the warehouse in the morning. Six sharp."

"Need me to bring anything? Extra supplies?"

"Naw, man. Just your brother, so he can help keep eyes on Jorge's and Juan Carlos' backs." I kept my eyes trained on the table, keeping Cindy in full view. "But make sure you're packin', both of you, because once the Mad Dog finds out Mina's double-crossing him—"

"—he's gonna lose his shit!"

"Yep." I ended the call with the tap of a finger, then pocketed my phone.

Never one to venture into another's business, I now found myself in a quandary.

Do I intervene, or shall I allow things to play out in the relatively public plight now unfolding on the floor of The Alchemist?

If I do nothing, then I'm condoning the manhandling of the girls in the club, which goes against Mina's strict policy—not to mention my morals. But if I intrude on a lover's quarrel unwanted, things could get ugly and out of hand fast.

One look in Cindy's eyes had me sliding off the barstool and stalking toward her.

Like a burning star, the woman always wore a beaming smile, making me wonder what flaming thoughts now went through her head. In all the time I'd known her, I'd never seen the slightest frown form on her lips. Even without a pout or downward turn of the corners of her mouth, her discomfort hit me with the same blunt force as if I'd slammed into a brick wall.

A montage of images flooded my head, and in each vivid memory, the little blonde, who the other employees had dubbed Malibu Barbie, wore a bright smile and bubbly, light-hearted disposition.

No one's ever that happy. Fuck no.

Most female employees talked about how Cindy had splendid hair, unblemished skin, impeccable teeth, the perfect body, and a picture-perfect life. But those were only what people saw on the surface, what Cindy allowed others to see. Or, perhaps, it's what others wanted to see when they looked upon her. I'd always felt the woman hid her real emotions from the group and the finer details of her life.

When I looked at her, I saw a woman naïve to the ways of the street, of the world—one who always tried to make peace, not war. Her ever-present smile left me to wonder what lay beneath the shell shrouding her with that happy façade, the one she wore like a second skin.

What makes you tick, mi pequeña paloma?

The nickname had come to me in a flash. And now, staring at her, the endearment *mi pequeña paloma*—my little dove—was only fitting since Cindy tried to sow peace rather than dissonance and disaccord.

Her blue eyes, now oceans of blustering emotions, revealed more to me in the last thirty seconds than I'd seen in the past six months. A mixture of anger, fear, despair, as well as a whole host of other emotions that flashed far too fast to catalog, now gleamed through the glossy hint of restrained tears in Cindy's eyes.

Slowly, and while keeping my eyes on Cindy, I made my way to the table.

"Everything okay over here?" I stood, ready to pounce if the fucker holding Cindy's bicep didn't release her.

"It's just a misunderstanding." Cindy nodded her head, sending blonde hair to swish around her shoulders. "He was just releasing me, right?"

Misunderstanding my ass, I thought to myself.

"Yeah," nodded Keegan, "we're all good over here." His Bostonian accent touched his words. "So, move along, tire-hugger."

"Tire-hugger?" I hadn't heard that slur since high school. "Man, I was born and raised right here in Texas, which is more than I can say for you, Masshole."

I didn't often use profanity in my verbalized speech—in my head was a whole other story—but the Massachusetts asshole always rubbed me the wrong way, him and his present company.

His lack of respect for Mexican Americans and Mexican nationals entering the US for a better life annoyed the fuck out of me. That and his disregard for anyone he deemed below him, regardless of race, ethnicity, or social and economic standing. But even that didn't bother me the same way his treatment of the opposite sex did. Not to mention how he treated women like objects or property to own instead of as actual human beings.

Yeah, that ignorant behavior had pissed me the fuck off on more than one occasion.

"Walk away." Keegan rose to full height.

Now, standing toe-to-toe with him, my eyes met his. It seemed the fucker, and I stood around the same height, but years of steroids, weightlifting, and football practice had put more bulk on his frame.

"Funny. I was about to tell you the same thing."

Ophelia approached the table, but she froze, balancing the drinks on the tray.

"Take them back to the bar," I said, addressing Ophelia. "They're on their way out."

"Well, fuck," whispered Ophelia. "There went my tip."

"Hey, I'm a paying customer." Keegan held a money clip fat with bills, chest level.

"I don't care what you are." My gaze flicked between his face and his hold on Cindy's arm. "Release her. It's time to go."

The self-righteous prick waved more old money

around than most banks had locked in their vaults. And it seemed he didn't know the definition of the word no.

A handful of seconds ticked by. The Masshole finally released Cindy, and she stepped behind me.

Smart move, mi pequeña paloma.

"Party's over." The fact she had willingly chosen my protection brought a slight grin to my lips without hesitation.

The fucker opened and closed his right fist, making me wonder when he'd strike.

"You and your friends need to pack it up." I waited for him to make the first move, which would only justify me tossing him out on his ass and banning him—him and his friends.

"You gonna make me, beaner?" He came inches from doing a chest bump as if testing the waters.

His little pussy friends giggled like school-children.

"Dude, seriously?" I held my ground, knowing full well. The moment he swung, I'd take him down like the little bitch he was, then I'd pound the fuck out of the next asshole who stepped forward.

"Guys, please." Cindy rushed forward, coming between Keegan and me. She pressed a hand to my chest.

Fuck. The girl should know better than to get involved.

With Cindy standing between his body and mine, the fucker took a cheap shot, knocking her down in the process. The fact that his action had slammed her to the ground and managed to make partial contact with my jaw ignited a fire deep inside me—one full of rage.

Cindy scrambled on her hands and knees, trying to avoid being stepped on.

I couldn't even afford to send a glance her way to make sure she was okay, because that'd only give Keegan an easy shot at me.

He took another swing, which only opened the door for me to beat the shit out of him. After all, he was on my turf and had touched one of the girls—*mi pequeña paloma*—my little dove.

3

Cindy

A searing heat ignited along the fingertips of my right hand, and a yelp ripped free from between my lips.

My left palm wrapped around Keegan's ankle, pushing him back, but he didn't budge a millimeter. If anything, he applied more pressure to my already aching digits.

"Please." The single word came out as a strangled cry. "You're hurting me."

"Get off her." Salvador shoved Keegan's chest.

The force made Keegan stumble, and he took a few steps back, falling against the table.

Now freed, I kneeled, keeping my hands off the floor.

"Stay out of the way." Salvador reached for me, pulled me to my feet, then dragged me behind him.

"You shouldn't have done that." Keegan lunged forward, leading with his right fist in a wide, wild swing.

Weeks of training with Dominic had my body falling into muscle memory.

Pivoting out of the way, I blocked the blow, then made a solid connection with Keegan's lower jaw. His knees buckled a bit as if he now stood on spaghetti legs, but then he recovered enough to swing again.

"Dude. Enough." Blocking his blow a second time, I kicked the back of his knee, sending him crashing to the floor with a heavy thud.

"You fuckin' Mexican." Spittle flew from his lips. "We're gonna—"

"—fuck you up," shouted Kyle Lubbock.

Benjamin Reid and Tobin Tilly rose from their chairs, then surrounded Salvador.

My heart pounded in my chest, and I stood there, unsure of what to do next.

"What the fuck's goin' on over here?" Clemente slid by me, breaking the circle, and Javier joined him. "Why weren't we invited to the fuckin' party?"

A glance over my shoulder revealed more men coming: Dominic, Spider, and Marciano.

"Damn," chimed in Marciano, his Italian accent thick. "Is it a full moon or something?"

"What?" Confusion slapped my reeling brain, and I cradled my hand to my chest.

Marciano's gaze flicked to my torn sleeve, and a frown marred his beautiful face.

"*Bello*, are you hurt?" Marciano eased his arms around my waist and ushered me away from the tables.

"No." I shook my head. "I'm okay."

Wiggling my fingers caused discomfort, but at least I could move them.

Twisting in his hold, I looked around his body to the fight unfolding.

"Salvador," I shouted, then pulled free. "Look out."

Somehow, Kyle had worked his way behind Salvador. And knowing Kyle the way I did, he was about to go in for a kidney punch.

A male patron sat at the table next to me. "I need this more than you." Grabbing his drink, I tightened my grip on the neck of the bottle. Pretending it was a baseball, I tossed it with a bit of a sideways slice.

The glass container twirled through the air, then smashed against Kyle's head.

"Damn, *Bello*." Marciano chuckled. "You've got an

arm on you, eh?" He raised his hand in the air, and on instinct, I high fived him.

Kyle went down with a groan.

That's what six years of practice out on the diamond field had done for me.

At least my father's money hadn't gone to total waste. I could still toss a ball or two, or in this case, a bottle. But any hope of joining the big leagues had dried up the moment my collarbone had snapped in two my senior year.

That unsanctioned outing had ended in a totaled vehicle, broken bones, one death, stitches for everyone else, and enough legal fees to put a few kids through college.

Once again, Marciano looped an arm around my waist, then walked me behind the bar with the other waitstaff.

"Don't move." Marciano's words came out firm and with an air of authority. "Do you hear me?"

I nodded, not sure if I could comply. After all, I was to blame for the fight unfolding in the club.

This is my fault.

"So." Ophelia leaned into me. "What the fuck did you do, Malibu?"

Sirens whined in the distance. They were faint, but from experience, it never took the police long to arrive once you could hear them. And when they arrived, that's when things would really get out of hand.

My father's gonna kill me.

"Leave me alone, Ophelia." I glared into her brown eyes. My smile now gone. "I'm not in the mood."

I shook my head. *Why can't this be a dream? Or a night terror?*

Keegan and his crew got off a handful of wild punches.

Great. This is just wonderful.

I fought back the tears threatening to burst free. If this gets back to my father, I won't hear the end of it.

No, not if, but when this gets back to my father, he's gonna flip out.

In no time at all, Salvador, Dominic, Spider, and the rest of the bouncers, like Clemente and Javier, had the jerks in arm holds. Dominic and the others escorted a now subdued Keegan and his friends past the bar and toward the front door.

Salvador approached. "I found this." He held the jewelry noose between his thumb and index finger.

The stone caught the overhead lights. Reflecting all the colors of the room, it sparkled like a prism, or a kaleidoscope.

Skirting past Marciano, I joined Salvador on the other side of the bar.

"I'll take that." I plucked the ring from his fingers.

"Where do you think you're going?" Salvador's brows shot upward.

As fast as my legs would take me, I made my way to the entrance.

Flashing lights from the parking police vehicles strobed through the open doorway.

"Don't let me see any of you here ever again." Dominic's heavy Russian accent thickened with each word he spoke. "Because we won't call the cops next time." He tapped Keegan's chest hard enough to make him stagger. "Understand?"

"Stop. Please." I squeezed past Dominic. "Wait. There's something I need to say to him—to Keegan."

"Make it quick," said Dominic, "the police are coming."

The officers had already exited their patrol vehicles, and now trekked through the parking lot, approaching the club.

"Just so we're clear on this point." Holding the ring up, I showed it to Keegan. "My answer is no, N-O. No." My voice rose a few octaves, losing the mellow control I had earlier in the evening. "No. I won't ever date you again." My hand shook along with the rest of my body. "No. I don't love—I *never* loved you."

I took in a ragged breath, then dropped the ring in the breast pocket of his long-sleeved, button-up shirt. Quickly, I drew my hand back as if the fabric had burned me.

"And for the record, Keegan, *no*, I won't marry you."

Salvador stood next to me. When my body swayed into his, he wrapped an arm around my waist.

The simplistic act drew Keegan's narrowed eyes to Salvador's hand now resting on my hip.

A comforting layer of warmth rose between my body and Salvador's, making me hyperaware of how close the two of us now stood.

"And just so you know, I already have my plus one for this year's firm party." With the comfort I drew from Salvador's warmth and support, I met Keegan's hardened gaze. "And it's not you."

"Are you telling me it's him?" Keegan scoffed.

"That's none of your concern." I knew full well that I shouldn't goad my ex, but I couldn't help it. Maybe if he thought I'd moved on, he'd leave me alone. "What if it is? I can take anyone I choose."

Salvador's unreadable gaze flicked to me for a split second, then returned to Keegan.

Oh, please, please, please, don't say anything. I chanted the words in my head, hoping the man went along with my little impromptu speech.

It was bad enough that I'd unwillingly dragged Salvador into a personal problem. Well, everyone at the bar into my issue. But now, I continued to pull him along for the mudslinging, roller coaster ride of my life.

"You'd choice this *Mexican* over me?" shouted Keegan. "What? Did you let him touch you? Fuck you?" A pulsing vein thumped on the side of his forehead.

Salvador released his hold on my hip. "Dude, don't speak to her that way."

His words took me by surprise. I'd never in my life had anyone come to my defense. So, it felt odd, and it left me on foreign ground.

My gallant protector's hand slid across my lower back. The contact of Salvador's fingertips along my bare skin ignited a wave of goose bumps that made me tremble with something other than hate.

Gazing at his profile, I took in the angular curves of his face.

Salvador's eyes held a cold steel bite to them as he stared at Keegan, but those same coppery brown irises of his, when they glanced my way, held a hint of something else—what, I wasn't sure.

"So, what, you're a whore now? Spreading your legs for everyone?" asked Keegan. "Is that it?" He lunged forward, reaching for me.

In a flash, Salvador stepped in front of me, shielding me yet again with his body.

"If you ever touch her again," Salvador grabbed Keegan by the throat, then slammed his body against the open door, "I'll—"

"Don't finish that comment, *esse*," stated Spider, who eased Salvador's hand off Keegan's neck. "Let the pigs in blue deal with him."

Four officers made their way up the ramp, then turned their attention to Dominic.

One of them looked vaguely familiar. I'd seen him inside the bar a few times, questioning Juan Carlos, Sonya, and Miss Mina Costa.

"Heard there was trouble tonight." Officer Rios' gaze bounced around the group. "So, I thought I'd come check it out."

Officer Rios' attention lingered a bit longer on Keegan, then stared at my torn sleeve and arm.

"Did one of these men touch you, Ma'am?" Officer Rios motioned to Keegan and his buddies, then he set an accusatory eye on Salvador, Dominic, and the rest of the men who had come to my aid.

"Yeah." Salvador nodded. "Keegan Black. He has no respect for women."

4

Salvador

Red, angry marks marred her creamy white skin, making my blood pressure rise.

Along with the ruddy coloration, yellow dime- to nickel-sized bruises dotted her bicep and shoulder.

Did her prick of an ex-boyfriend do that?

It was a question I'd need to ask *mi pequeña paloma*, my little dove. If so, that'd give me one more reason to pound the shit out of Keegan the next time he popped up on my radar.

As my grandfather always said, nothing ranks lower in life than a coward who touches a woman in order to feel like a man.

"Hey, you okay?" I pressed a hand to her lower

back, then coaxed her away from the interior of the club, leaving the loud music behind.

"Yeah." That happy-go-lucky façade slipped into place. "I'm good. Thanks for asking." Her eyes darted in my direction. "How about you?"

"I'm good. Let's take a break, shall we?" I made my way to the closed off club patio, still under renovation, then unclipped the partition band. "After you."

At my invitation, she eased past me, then took a seat on a bench in the corner.

She tipped her head back, gazing at the night sky. Slowly, she filled her lungs, only to exhale at an even slower rate. Under the dim light of the outside streetlamps, her chest rose and fell with each deep breath she took. The motion drew my eyes to her upper body, or more precisely, the soft mounds of her breasts, shielded by the fitted blouse hugging her every curve.

Fuck. I rubbed my jaw. *What am I doing?*

She was off limits. One of Miss Costa's employees.

Another one of my grandfather's old sayings came to mind.

You don't shit where you eat.

It wasn't as if it mattered. The girl was way outta my league. It wasn't as if she'd see anything in me.

And I'd be a fool to think that someone like her would want to date a nobody like me.

I'll only taint her, stain her with the sins of my past, present, and those to come.

"What a day, huh?" She leaned back, eyes closed.

"Do they hurt?"

"Huh? What?" Her lids sprung open.

"Those." I pointed to her bicep, drawing her eyes to the fresh angry marks.

"Oh, uhm, no." She shook her head. "They're nothing." A light blush covered her face. "Since I'm light-complected, I mark easily. That's all. They'll go away soon."

"And what about these?" I skimmed a finger over a few of the yellowish bruises marring her smooth skin. "Did he do that to you?"

"N-no." A wave of goose bumps erupted the length of her arm. "I, uhm, I'm clumsy sometimes." She avoided my gaze. "Run into walls, furniture, doors, and stuff, that's all."

"You don't say?"

"Yeah." Cindy nodded, but I wasn't sold on her fabricated words.

The woman walked with an elegant grace, and I'd never seen her bump into walls or anything else during her shifts at the club. And while at work, she seemed to display a spatial awareness of items within her near vicinity. So, for her to state the bruises were a direct result of clumsy behavior, well, didn't bode well.

For now, I'd let the topic go. However, if the bruising continued, I'd need to bring it up to Mina Costa.

She studied me with an astute intent, then her eyes widened.

"Is that—"

Her blonde eyelashes fluttered, sending shadows dancing across her cheeks.

"What?" I held her wide-eyed, innocent gaze.

"Is that b-blood?" She raised her arm, then placed the tips of her fingers on the side of my jaw. Slowly, she turned my head, then leaned in for a closer inspection.

Her feather-light touch set my skin on fire, and the subtle floral perfume she wore drew me closer to her. So close, I could almost taste her lips.

The aroma of the fragrance had an odd, almost calming effect.

She exhaled and her warm breath blew over my skin, sending my heart pounding in my chest.

Tonight, seeing Keegan put his hands on her, woke the rage monster inside of me. The second he touched her, it was as if a switch had flipped inside of me. And in that moment, all I wanted to do was pound the shit out of him.

"Your nose is, uhm, it's . . ."

Her lower lip quivered, and she rubbed her hands together.

I swiped at the skin directly below my nose but above my lip, and that's when I saw it between my fingers—the red crimson color of blood.

That fucker, Kyle, had sucker-punched me in the nose.

"It's nothing." I waved it off. "I've had far worse."

Silence settled, thick and heavy, in the space between the two of us.

Thoughts of her slipping the ring inside Keegan's pocket came to mind.

"That was a big rock." I changed the topic of discussion.

"Not big enough." Her words came out dry and monotone.

"Excuse me?"

Was she implying that if the caret count had gone up that she would've closed the deal?

"Don't look at me like that." She rubbed her eyes.

"Like what?"

"Like I'm some kind of gold-digging plastic bitch." She huffed a sigh.

"Didn't know I was." I held her gaze, taking notice

of the turmoil swirling in the ocean blue color. "Wasn't my intention."

"Good." She sat in defiance. "Because I'm not what they say I am. I'm not."

Her back remained ramrod straight and the mask she usually wore over her face slipped a bit, revealing an array of emotions, and of those, a hurt defensiveness flashed the strongest.

"You're not what?" Now I had a need to know.

"An emotionless Malibu Barb—never mind." She waved me off as if to dispel her comment. "Just forget I said anything."

Once again, that fake, warm but impersonal smile touched her lips. But the pain in her eyes remained bright, drawing me to her.

What makes you tick, mi pequeña paloma?

"Why do you do it?"

"Do what?" Confusion knitted her blonde brows together.

"Hide behind the persona the others refer to you as?"

Her manicured brows shot up, animating her deadpan expression.

"Because it's what they want to see, and it's easier that way." Cindy rose, then headed down the walk toward the entrance of the club. "People will always see what they want." She glanced over her shoulder as if to see if I followed. "And no matter what I do or say, they'll never see anything different." Her words dripped with raw emotion. "They'll never see me."

"I do." I reached for her hand, clasping it between both of mine.

"What?" She came to a complete stop.

Her hand fit inside of mine, and I laced my fingers with hers. "I see you."

For a moment, it seemed as if time ticked slower. Even the thump of the band's live base inside fell away.

"There you are, *Bello.*" Marciano's voice crooned in the night air. "Found you at last."

The Italian's words broke the silent serenity that had settled between Cindy and me. With reluctance, I released her hand.

"Didn't know I was lost." Once again, that plastic smile surfaced, making me crave what she kept hidden underneath.

"Well, it seems I wasn't the first to find you." A grin split Marciano's lips.

"I guess not." Her nervous gaze flicked between his and mine.

"Now," he stretched out the single word. "Is it true?"

"Is what true?" She kept her voice calm and even-toned.

"That he's your plus one to the much-anticipated Stevens and Black gala event?"

"A what?" I tried to focus on his words but found my need to not let her out of my sight, distracting.

"A gala," he said with a chuckle, "as in a ball."

"I'd hardly call it a ball," she replied. "It's more of a pat-yourself-on-the-back event with a heavy dose of *I'll scratch your back if you scratch mine* in a convoluted manner."

5

Cindy

"You don't have to go with me." I felt childish for even implying Salvador was my plus one. "People show up to these events alone all the time."

"Oh, *Bello*," said Marciano. "If your *savior* finds himself busy, I'll fill in. I wouldn't mind rubbing elbows with some of Dallas' elitists."

"I never said I wouldn't go." Salvador opened the club door, then waited for me to enter.

"But you never said you would, either." Marciano winked at Salvador. "So, which is it? Are you going or not?"

"What are ya'll talking about?" Ophelia approached, holding the hostess clipboard in hand.

"Oh, we're just discussing who's taking Cindy to the Stevens and Black gala." Marciano offered me his arm, and the moment I took it, he whisked me away from a group of mingling guest.

"Hey, wait, I don't want this fuckin' list," shouted Ophelia, holding the clipboard over her head. "This is your job, Malibu."

Halfway across the dance floor, a sea of arms and legs and big hair swallowed Ophelia's disgruntled comments, as well as Salvador's image from view.

"Where are you taking me?" I had to yell the words, and even then, I wasn't sure if the Italian heard me.

Once on the other side of the room, he pulled me into one of the side offices, then shut the door. Movement in the back drew my attention, and my body stiffened.

"Relax, *Bello*," whispered Marciano. "It's only Filipe and Spider. You're among friends."

My breaths came in shallow puffs. "What . . . w-why am I in here?"

"We can't have you out on the floor like this." Marciano wiggled the torn fabric of my sleeve. "Plus, we wanted to make sure you're okay."

"I'm, uhm, I'm good. Honestly, guys." I released Marciano's arm. "I gotta go back to work."

"Not like this, *Bello*," said Marciano.

Once again, he toyed with the torn sleeve.

Filipe sprung from his seat. "I have a sewing kit in my car."

"Of course you do," said Spider from the corner of the room.

"I'll be back." Filipe brushed by Marciano, and the two men exchanged looks.

In no time at all, Filipe returned with a zipper pouch full of sewing items and accessories: everything from needles to tiny colorful thread spools along with buttons and snaps.

"Hold still, *Bello*." Marciano held a threaded needle in hand. "I don't want to poke you."

Not gonna lie, being in the room with the men, well, Spider, did my head in. The man looked lethal at every angle viewed.

"Are you about done?" I asked, glancing at the sleeve that my impromptu Italian seamstress had tacked in place.

"Almost." Marciano concentrated on the task of stitching the fabric together, and if, being honest, he'd done a damn fine job so far.

Filipe leaned on the table next to where I sat, watching.

"Where'd the old bruises come from?" asked Filipe, as if the direction the conversation had turned was a normal, everyday topic. "Did someone—"

As soon as he spoke the words, Spider's head whipped back. "Someone touch her?" He slid his phone in his pocket, rose, then headed in my direction.

"Look." I held my hands up. "It's not what ya'll are thinkin'—any of you."

Inside the room with the three of them, I felt an odd sort of comfort that they cared enough to ask. But that didn't keep the walls from feeling as if they now creeped closer, inch-by-inch, bringing on a sensation of claustrophobia.

Spider came to a full stop next to me. His arms crisscrossed over his broad chest while his eyes zoomed in on my arm.

"And what do you think we're thinking, *Bello*?" Marciano knotted the thread, then used a miniature pair of scissors to trim the line close to the seam.

"Miss Stevens to the hostess desk," Ophelia's voice crackled over the intercom speaker in the room. "Cindy Stevens, you're needed at the hostess desk."

"I, uhm." Pulling away from Marciano, I walked around Spider. "They need me out there."

I made a mad dash for the door.

"Thanks for fixing me up," I blurted out. "Thanks for everything." I slipped out of the room.

"*Bello*, come back," said Marciano, but the chatter out on the floor swallowed his voice.

The moving sea of arms and legs swallowed me, and I weaved in and out and between dancing bodies. By the time I reached the hostess desk, my heart hammered so hard in my chest, it sounded like another track layer of base the band had laid down with the current beat playing.

"You owe me, Malibu." Ophelia shoved the clipboard against my chest, then stormed. "And big."

"I'm s-sorry." I glanced at the line of patrons forming next to the desk.

"Sorry doesn't make up for the tips I lost doing your fuckin' job, now does it?" She stormed off.

Her words came out with a shortness I could only describe as 'mean girl bitchiness,' which Ophelia had down pat.

A glance at the watch on my wrist assured me that I had two more hours of meet-n-greet, so I wore my best smile and greeted the next person in line.

"Howdy, ya'll. Welcome to The Alchemist." I motioned for the man and woman holding hands to follow me. "Boy, you two make a cute couple. Let's find ya somethin' romantic, like in the balcony section, shall we?"

Lickety-split. I had the love birds seated, then went to work on whittling down that line. The time went by fast enough, and it helped that I kept myself busy. While I worked, I caught glimpses of the guys keeping an eye on me, which I found comforting.

Once the bar shut and The Alchemist was void of patrons, I headed for the employee lockers to grab my stuff.

"Where'd you park?" asked Salvador.

A little yelp passed between my lips.

"Goodness me." I held my chest. "You nearly made me jump outta my skin."

"Sorry. Didn't mean to scare you." He leaned against the locker next to mine.

"No worries. I'm a bit jumpy these days." A genuine smile played on my lips. "I wanted to tell you again how much I appreciated what you did today. Comin' to my aid."

"No apology needed. It's what I do."

"I know that." A wave of heat swept across my chest, over my neck, then spilled onto my face. "Just the same, thanks for stickin' up for me and all."

"So, about my question . . ."

"What?"

"Your car." He held my gaze. "Where'd you park it?"

"Oh, uhm, on the side of the building." I grabbed

my purse, then shut my locker. "In the employee parking area. Why?"

"Hey, Sal," shouted Clemente. "Help me carry a keg to the bar."

"Get Javier or Filipe to help you."

"They're already taking care of the other one," replied Clemente.

"Fine. I'll be there in a minute, Clem." His gaze stayed glued on me. "Wait for me by the entrance, and I'll walk you out."

"That's not necessary." I gave him a smile, then shouldered the strap of my purse. "I'm good. Night."

I headed for the hallway, but he stepped in front of me, then placed a hand on my forearm. Not hard like Keegan often did, but gentle like. The warmth of his touch gave me goose-pimpled flesh.

"Don't go out alone." His voice took a commanding tone that made my stomach flip-flop. "Wait for me." He released his hold. "Understand?"

The moment his hand left my body, a sense of loss registered.

"Uh-huh." I nodded, unable to vocalize anything else, then shot out into the hallway as fast as I could.

Halfway across the open floor plan of the main floor of the club, I spotted Ophelia and her crew, so I slowed my pace. At the bar, I slid my purse off my shoulder, plopped it on top of the smooth surface, then fished for my keys and phone.

A quick glance at the screen of my cell revealed more than a dozen calls from Keegan, a handful from an unknown number—more than likely Keegan again—then a couple of text messages from my father about the upcoming firm gala. His instructions came across loud, clear, and precise. I was to go to Urea's Bridal shop to select one of the designated dress designs in white this year with a pastel trim of any color.

He does this every year, forces the three of us to dress with a similar theme and color: my mother, him, and me.

A tinge of anger reignited, souring my mood.

I'm sick of it. Sick of people telling me what to do. Sick of constantly feeling judged. Sick of certain somebodies dictating who I am—or should be.

My gaze flicked to the door. Ophelia and her little "mean girl crew" had already vacated the building, so I headed for the exit.

Once outside, a steady breeze blew hard enough to make the trees sway in the dark. Drawing in a deep breath, I drew in the surrounding air. A hint of pre-rain tickled my nose, and I glanced overhead at the star-dotted sky.

Some cumulonimbus clouds, nimbus for short,

hung low, illuminated by the full moon, creating an overcast.

I loved the rain, had ever since I could remember. The event always brought with it a peacefulness that only the calming raindrops on a windowsill could offer. It made me feel cozy, content even, and it created an inner peace for me.

Maybe it's because rain was a symbol of cleansing and clarity. And about right now, in my life, I could use a lot of both.

The corner parking lot streetlight lit up my car, casting shadows over it. Something seemed off, and the closer I came to my vehicle, I knew why—the front sat way too low to the ground.

"Seriously?" A heavy sigh left my lips, and I squeezed my eyes shut for a couple of seconds.

How does one end up with not only one but two flat tires?

"Need a ride?" Keegan's shadow snaked out of the darkness, making me jump.

"Uhm, no." I shook my head. "I'm good. I'll get an Uber."

"At this hour? Naw, I'll take you home." He approached, blocking my path back to the club.

"I said n-no, Keegan."

He took several steps toward me, and I countered

with the same amount back until pressed against the hood of my car.

"Hey." Salvador's single word contained an eerie calmness. "The lady said no." He crossed the parking lot, heading in my direction. "And that trespass citation the police handed out earlier went into effect right then and there. So, get off the property."

Clemente, Javier, Filipe, Marciano, and Spider came into view, and the minute they started walking to my car, Keegan got inside his Ford Mustang, then sped out of the parking lot.

"You two okay?" Spider kneeled next to one of my front tires.

"Yeah," said Salvador. "We're good."

"Well, if you call two flat tires good, then yeah, we're good." I let out a shaky breath, glad that Keegan had left.

"Clem and I can take care of the flats in the morning," said Javier. "Get 'em patched for ya."

"They'll need more than a patch job." Spider peeled back a loose flap of tread from the tire.

"What? Why?" I asked.

"Because someone sliced your tires." Spider rose.

6

Salvador

"Why does he—" Cindy huffed. "What makes him think this is okay?" Her words left her lips as a soft, shaky whisper.

"Because Keegan's an ass," replied Clemente.

"Naw, what'd Sal call that fucker?" Chuckled Javier.

"Masshole," I replied.

"Yeah." Nodded Clemente. "That's it. He's a fuckin' Masshole."

"Come on." I motioned to Cindy. "I'll give you a ride home."

"Are you sure you don't mind?" Her gaze darted around everywhere but on me.

"Don't mind at all."

"Toss me her keys," shouted Javier. "And I'll have my cousin, Pablo, give it a once over to make sure everything's good."

"That's not necessary. I can—"

I plucked the keys out of her hand, then tossed them. "Heads up."

Javier caught them in his right hand, then headed for his SUV. The others followed him.

"I got shotgun," shouted Marciano.

"Get in the back." Spider yanked Marciano out of the way.

The two men grappled, but the moment Spider wrapped an arm around Marciano's neck, holding him in a headlock, the younger Italian relented.

"Fine," Marciano said with what looked like a pout. "Take it if it's that important to you, old man."

In no time at all, the SUV started, and the tail-lights blinked out of view.

"Come on." I nudged her. "Let's go before the rain hits."

She followed me to the side of the building where I had parked my motorcycle.

"Wait." Her eyes grew large. "Where's your Jeep?"

"At home." I patted the seat.

"What? No." She shook her head. "I can't ride that."

"Why not?"

"Because it's not safe. That's why." She stood with her hands on her hips. "I'll just call an Uber."

"I assure you, it's safe." I handed her my helmet. "Put it on."

She stood there, holding the helmet in one hand and her phone in the other, with a stunned look on her face.

"Don't tell me you've never ridden on one before." I walked around the back of my bike and lowered the rider foot pegs.

"Nope." She shook her head. "Never have, and I'm not starting now."

Cindy tried to give me the helmet back, but I didn't bite.

"Well, you don't know what you're missing."

I sat on the seat of my bike, placed my hands on the handlebars, balanced the body, engaged the break with my right hand to keep it from rolling forward, then swept the kickstand with my left foot.

"No. I'm good." She unlocked the screen of her cell, then groaned. "Ugh."

"What's wrong?" My gaze swept over the curves of her body.

"My phone's about to die." She huffed. "It's got like two percent on it. Can I use yours?"

"Uh-uh." I patted the seat behind me. "Get on."

"But I don't—"

"You live what, less than ten minutes away from here?" I asked.

"How do you know that?"

"I run security checks on everyone for Miss Costa."

"Oh." She chewed on her lower lip.

"Come on, get on. Besides, by the time you request an Uber, and it gets here, you could already be home. I'll even go slow just for you. Promise."

"You won't go fast?" She held the helmet with one hand and rubbed her arm with the other.

"Naw." I flipped the kickstand, then got off the bike.

Slowly, I approached her, reading the nervous clues of her body language.

"Do you trust me?" Unzipping my jacket, I slid it off.

"Yes." Her response came without any hesitation.

"Good." I handed her my jacket. "Here, put this on, so you're not cold."

I didn't bother to tell her the jacket offered a layer of protection for motorcyclists since that news might only spook her more.

"Let me hold those for you." I eased the helmet from her hand and the purse from her shoulder. "I'll put your bag in one of the saddlebags."

"Thanks." Slowly, she slid my jacket on.

Her eyes followed my movement. I set the helmet on the seat, then secured her purse inside the leather compartment.

The leather cuffs of my jacket covered the tips of her fingers, so I rolled them up, giving her full use of her hands.

Once she had it on, I zipped it, then placed the helmet on her head, making sure it fit snug. My hand skimmed across her neck, touching her soft, flawless skin.

She sucked in a breath, then bit down on her bottom lip. Goose bumps erupted across her exposed flesh, and a little mew escaped her mouth.

Seems my little dove's nervous. A grin tugged at my lips.

"You okay?" I took her hand in mine.

"Uh-huh." She nodded.

"You see these?" I pointed to the pegs, and she nodded. "After I sit down, and only when I tell you to, you're going to put your right foot on this peg, place your hand on my shoulder, swing your left leg over the bike, then rest it on the peg on the other side. Once you've done all that, you'll sit down right here." My fingers drummed against the seat. "Got it?"

"I uhm, I think so."

"Come here." I guided her to my motorcycle.

Again, I sat down, grabbed the handlebars, employed the front brake with my right hand so the bike wouldn't roll forward, swept the kick stand, shifted to first, then glanced at her.

"Okay. Get on."

I offered her my left hand, and the moment she took it, I set her palm on my shoulder.

"Right foot on the peg," I said, giving her verbal directions to follow. "Swing the other leg over. Left foot on the peg. Sit down."

As soon as she sat, I gripped both of her knees, pressing them to my body.

"Keep them like this," I said, and my hands lingered longer than they should have .

"Wait." Her voice squeaked. "You don't have a helmet."

"You're wearing it." I chuckled. "Don't worry. I'm fine." I patted her left knee.

She wiggled on the seat, trying to slide as far back and away from my body as possible, which made me grin.

"Give me your hands."

"Why?"

"So, I can show you where to hold on."

She held her arms next to the sides of my body. I took her hands in mine, tugged her forward, then placed her hands on my upper abdomen.

48

"You can hold me here," I said, then still holding her hands, I then flattened her palms against the gas can. "When I'm coming to a stop, press your hands here to brace yourself."

"Brace myself? Why?"

"It'll keep you from pushing me forward and, well"—there was no easy way to say it—"so, I don't smash my nuts against the tank."

"Oh," the single word came out in a cute little squeak.

Engaging the motor, my baby purred to life. My left hand eased off the clutch a bit, taking me into that friction zone.

"Hold on to me," I shouted over the sound of the engine.

She yelped, then grabbed onto my shoulders.

"My waist, not my arms or shoulders." I resisted the urge to laugh.

Complying, she slid her hands down my back, but then she latched onto the sides of my shirt.

Taking hold of first her right hand, I pulled it around my waist, then did the same with the left.

"You're gonna want to scoot closer to my body, Cindy." This time, I couldn't keep the light chuckle out of my voice. "I don't bite. I promise."

She inched a bit closer, but still remained too far away.

So, I shifted into first, then engaged the throttle with my right hand. Slowly, I increased the momentum of the bike, giving her time to adjust to the feel and movement.

The moment the motorcycle moving caused her body to lunge forward, another little yelp left her lips. She wrapped her arms around my waist, and her body slid into mine, molding against me.

"Hold on tight," I said over my shoulder.

I crossed the parking lot, taking it slow, then came to the main road.

"Move with my body," I shouted. "If I lean right or left, you lean too—never against me. Got it?"

"I think so," her voice barely hit my ear.

The moment I turned onto the street, she tightened her hold, pressing her upper body and thighs against me.

"Relax." I glanced at her, but only saw the top of the helmet covering her head. "Enjoy the ride. I promise, you're safe with me."

She shook at first, but once on the main road, Cindy relaxed a bit. Somewhere along the way, her hands had slipped under my shirt, making me hyperaware of the skin-on-skin contact.

Not gonna lie. I liked the feel of her body molded intimately to mine, not to mention the heat of her touch.

I slowed at an intersection, then stopped at a red light. She wiggled behind me.

"Stop bouncing around." I looked over my shoulder and locked gazes with her. "And *don't* take your feet off the pegs."

7

Cindy

The rumble between my legs made me feel alive.

Never in a million years had I thought that I'd ever sit on a motorcycle, much less ride on one. And somehow, sharing this first with Salvador seemed only fitting after today's events.

When he had asked me if I trusted him earlier, I surprised myself by responding as fast as I had. But in truth, I did trust him because the man made me feel safe. Plus, earlier, when Keegan had acted up in the club, he came to my aid without delay.

Salvador eased into a turn. I leaned with him, following his body movement with ease. The simplistic act felt so natural.

Somewhere along the ride in the dark, my fingers had found their way under his shirt. Each time his abs contracted, his rock-hard muscles moved under my fingertips. A desire to feel more of his skin—to feel his body, flesh-to-flesh with mine, had parts of me reacting in ways I hadn't expected.

A growing heat spread between my legs, along with a dampness that surprised me. Sure, I'd read about how some women reacted sexually to a man in fictionalized stories in books before, but this was new territory for me. It was most certainly not a sensation I'd ever experienced with Keegan, and since I'd only had one sexual partner, I had nothing else to compare it to. But I knew one thing, I liked it.

What does that say about me? I exhaled a heavy sigh.

The motorcycle slowed, and Salvador looked over his shoulder.

"You okay back there?" His voice made me jump.

"Yeah. I'm good." I squeezed him tighter.

A stop sign came into view. Two vehicles, one across the street, and one to the left, stopped, then seconds later, the motorcycle came to a full stop.

My body slid forward, and Salvador groaned.

"Loosen your hold." He tapped my left hand with his. "And when we brake, press your hands here." Salvador placed my left palm against the gas tank.

"Then when we take off, you can hold me again. Okay?"

"Yeah. Sorry."

The car opposite Salvador and me drove straight. Whereas the truck to the left turned in front of where we both waited at the stop sign. Darkness had swallowed up the street, and with the truck's windows tinted, its windows looked black, making it impossible to see the driver as well as if any passengers rode inside.

A sensation of eyes roaming over my body made me shiver, and for some odd reason, I turned away from the truck, shielding my face from the shine of the vehicle's headlights.

"Scoot back onto your seat."

When I did, he eased his body back.

"I can go back further." At least I hoped I could without my butt falling off.

"Naw." He squeezed my left knee. "You're good where you are."

The contact sent a wave of goose bumps rushing across the length of my body, making my nipples tingle, then harden. And in that moment, I was thankful for the leather jacket pressed between my body and his.

"I turn right, yes?" he asked.

"Uh-huh," was all I managed to squeak out.

"Hold on."

My hands slid over his ribbed abdomen, and I closed my eyes, enjoying the feel of his warm, inviting flesh. Drawing in a deep breath, I breathed in his masculine scent: a mixture of sandalwood, vanilla, and something in the citrus family that I couldn't pinpoint, along with a hint of either scotch or gin from working behind the bar.

Mmm. My new favorite smell. A smile played on my lips for a few seconds, then I shook my head. *What am I doing?*

It wasn't as if someone like Salvador would ever look at a person like me.

I'm not his type.

But then again, I didn't ever recall seeing him with anyone, ever.

What if he's married? I scolded myself. *And here I am, drooling over him like a prized choice steak.*

An impulse to say a few Hail Mary's came to mind, and I wasn't even a Catholic.

Objectifying him. Lusting after him. Coveting what I don't have.

Yeah, I'd broken a few commandments and committed a couple of sins since sliding on the back of the bike and holding on to him.

The motorcycle came to a full stop. Salvador placed a hand over mine. His thumb rubbed against my fingers, making the skin extra sensitive to the touch.

"Hold on to my shoulder and swing your leg over."

Doing as instructed, I climbed off and instantly missed the feel of his body pressed against mine.

He swept the kick stand, flicking it down, then got off the motorcycle.

An adrenaline thrill rippled through me at the thought of what I'd just done.

I rode on the back of a motorcycle, a real motorcycle.

The thought blew my mind.

If my parents had known what I had just done, well, my mother would've given me one of those looks of hers—the one that always had a way of speaking volumes.

And my father . . . he'd just yell at me, expressing his displeasure at my life choices.

In his eyes, I never do anything right—never.

Salvador retrieved my purse.

"I'll walk you to the door." He glanced at the townhome I called home. "It's dark. You don't leave a light on?"

"Oh, uhm, that's weird. They're on a timer." I unzipped his jacket.

"Well, that doesn't explain why it's dark." He walked a few steps in front of me. "Hand me your key."

"There isn't one."

"What?"

"It's a keyless lock." I approached the keypad and pressed my thumb against the reader in the middle. "Do you want to come in for a moment?"

Two audible beeps sounded, then the gears whirled, unlocking the door.

"Sure." He nodded.

Darkness consumed the entry, and I stepped over the threshold with Salvador on my heels. I slid a hand along the wall, mentally counting the steps from the front door to the light switch. Something crunched under my shoes. Two steps later, I slipped, sliding across the floor in a makeshift split.

A yelp left my lips.

Strong arms wrapped around my body, keeping me upright and on my feet.

"Careful," whispered Salvador next to my ear. "The floor's wet."

I found the light switch and flicked the lever, illuminating the entrance and half of the living room.

"Oh, no." A gasp left my lips.

Tears stung my eyes, and a shudder shook my

body. Kneeling, I stared at my babies lying motion-less on the floor.

"What was in the wall tank, Cindy?" Salvador gingerly walked over the water-soaked floor and entered the living room.

"My dwarf seahorses." I stifled a sob at their little bodies. Most still clutched the macro-algae seaweed. "Why would someone do this?"

Salvador disappeared from view. Then, when he came back, he took the stairs to the second floor, two at a time. His phone sat cradled between his ear and shoulder. He rattled off the address, then paused at the top of the stairs.

"The police are on their way," he said, then disap-peared from view for less than twenty seconds.

"Wait? What?" Confusion set in. His words didn't make any sense.

Why are the police coming? My heart pounded in my chest.

"They can't. Please, you don't understand." A tightness overcame my chest, restricting my breaths.

My gaze roamed over the living room, trying to make sense of the overturned furniture and broken debris. Several words covered one of the walls in bold, black letters: *slut, whore, bitch, and hoe.*

The other wall contained a few phrases: *I'll be*

back; I'm coming for you; you're mine; you can run, but you can't hide.

The pounding of Salvador's footsteps echoed in the stairwell.

"My father . . ."

My legs felt wobbly, and I staggered, slamming into the wall.

A tingling sensation made the tips of my fingers prickle, and the room swam around me like a waterspout.

"Hey." Salvador approached. "Look at me."

He wrapped an arm around my waist and drew me to his body. With one hand, he cupped my chin, tilting my head until his eyes locked with mine.

"Take slow, deep breaths through your nose." He demonstrated the motion. "Then exhale slowly." Once again, he went through the motions.

After filling my lungs several times, the fog clouding my vision vanished, leaving tears to blur everything in my viewing field.

He cradled me to his chest, holding me in a firm embrace.

Sirens pierced the darkness outside the open door, followed by strobing lights. Burying my face against his chest, I sobbed.

"It's gonna be okay," he whispered in my ear.

"No. You don't understand." I shook my head, knowing full well the depths of the wrath coming my way. "He's going to be mad—really mad." My teeth chattered.

"I got you, *mi pequeña paloma.*"

8

Salvador

"She can't stay here during an active investigation." Officer E. Hager, badge number 4826, motioned to Cindy, who sat curled up on a porch swing. "Is there somewhere she can go for a few days? Family? Friends? Her parents?" He handed me a card.

"Yeah." I nodded. "I can take her to a hotel. Or to her parents if she wants."

Cindy's eyes widened. "No. Not there." She shook her head. "I don't want you to take me."

"You don't want to go where?" The officer kneeled in front of her.

"To my parents' home." Her fair skin looked more pale than usual, which I didn't think could happen.

And what little color she had left drained from her face.

"Then you don't have to go there." I reached for her hand. "I can take you—"

"Back up." The officer's voice grew thick and deep.

His partner, J. Goss—badge number 9832— stepped in front of me. "Son, you need to wait over there." He motioned to one of three police vehicles. The other two officers remained in the house, looking around.

"Why?" I asked, trying to contain my annoyance.

"Because my partner needs to talk to Miss Stevens alone." Officer Goss gestured toward the black and white marked SUVs once again. "How about you and I have a little talk about what happened earlier at The Alchemist." He cleared his throat. "Were you involved in that? Did you harass Miss Stevens?"

"Man, you got it all wrong." I shook my head, then headed to the first of the two SUVs.

"Then how about you set me straight?" He stood in front of me, blocking my view of Cindy. "How do you know her?"

"I work at The Alchemist." I crossed my arms over my chest.

"Yasmina Ona Costa owns the place, right?"

"Yes, Sir."

"So, you work for her."

"Yes. Sir."

"Then you know of her ties to the Mexican Cartel, then? To her uncle, Joaquin Costa."

"No, Sir."

"Is that a no to the cartel ties or knowing her uncle?"

"No, Sir," I repeated the phrase, knowing it annoyed the fuck out of him. "I don't know her uncle personally. Don't know what her relationship is with the man. And I don't know of any ties my employer has with the cartel."

Officer Goss' face turned a ruddy red. "Were you at work with Miss Stevens this afternoon—this evening?"

"Yes, Sir." I nodded, keeping my answers as short as possible because I didn't want to give him any ammunition to use later.

"Is that yours?" Officer Goss did a head nod toward my motorcycle.

"Yes, Sir." I held the man's gaze.

"How about some ID," said Officer Goss. "You got some on ya?"

"Yes, Sir." Slowly, I reached for my wallet, then handed the officer my identification.

It seemed I was now to undergo a third questioning session by police today: first at the bar, second time by Officer Hager, and now Officer Goss was barking up my ass.

"Mr. Vargas," Officer Hager called my name, then waved to me. "Come over here and join us." His gaze flicked to his partner.

I made my way across the yard with Officer Goss on my ass. Once on the porch, I stood with an open stance, waiting to see what the fuck was going to happen now.

"Miss Stevens just informed me that you two are dating." Officer Hager held my gaze in what looked more like a challenge than a question.

Keeping my expression neutral, I nodded. "Yes, Sir."

Oh, *mi pequeña paloma*, what have you started now?

"Is that so?" asked Officer Goss.

"Yes, Sir." I nodded once more, and this time, I even gave the officer a warm, friendly fuck-off smile. Seconds later, I schooled my face into an emotionless mask.

"Miss Stevens stated she arrived on the premises with you this evening," said Officer Hager.

"Yes. Sir." I didn't move a muscle.

"I see only one helmet over there, Son. And two

of you." Officer Hager pointed at my motorcycle. "Is that all you got?"

"Yes, Sir." I wanted to tell the fucker I had extra helmets at home, but at this stage of the game, it seemed mote at best to bring it up. So, I stuck to the plan of answering the officer's closed-ended questions with a simple yes and no responses.

"Are you aware of Texas helmet laws?" asked Officer Goss.

"Yes, Sir."

"Then why don't you tell me what you know of that law, boy?"

"Yes, Sir," I said, holding his gaze. "If a motorcyclist is over the age of twenty, possesses a trained motorcycle operator license, and contains at least ten thousand in medical insurance coverage, the rider isn't required to wear a helmet. And Sir, I meet all three of those Texas law requirements."

"Look, Salvador gave me a ride because someone slashed my tires at The Alchemist." My little dove had finally found her voice and spoke. "He had one helmet with him, because he wasn't expecting to have a passenger today." She kept the tone of her voice smooth and calm. "And he let me wear the helmet."

Her eyes contained a glossy sheen from crying

prior, but the depths of despair and fear I'd seen earlier in them hadn't yet fully vanished.

"So, how long have you and Miss Stevens been dating?" asked Officer Hager.

Thoughts of the prior altercation with Keegan at the bar came to mind. She'd broken up with him around two weeks ago, or so she had said.

"Couple of weeks," I replied, hoping my story matched her fabricated one.

"You're a man of few words, aren't ya, Son?" Officer Goss handed me my identification, and I put it back in my wallet.

"Yes, Sir."

A set of headlights flashed across the yard, blinding me. Seconds later, the lights turned off. It was then I realized another police vehicle had arrived.

"Homicide's here to sweep the house." Officer Goss headed to the new arrivals. "I'll brief them."

"Officer." Cindy stifled a yawn. "Am I needed any further? Either one of us?"

"No, Ma'am." Officer Hager turned to face me. "And she's staying with you at your place?"

My little dove nodded, making me wonder exactly what she had told the officer.

"Yes, Sir." At this point, my answers remained on autopilot.

"You have my card if anything comes up," said Officer Hager. "We'll be in touch."

"Yes, Sir." I extended an arm, shook the man's hand, then turned to Cindy, offering her some assistance.

The woman looked pale, dead tired, and her eyes and nose had turned red from crying earlier. I wanted nothing more than to hold her, comfort her, and put a smile back on her lips.

She slipped her hand on mine. I drew her to her feet, then into my arms for a hug, which she fell into with a natural grace. Her arms looped around me, and her body intimately molded to mine. And as sure as fuck. My cock stirred, drawn to the warmth of her body.

Officer Hager continued to watch my interaction with Cindy. It made me wonder if the ass now looked for any cracks in her story.

I'm not gonna lie. Holding her in my arms felt good, especially since she sought me out. And even if she only sought comfort from a fake boyfriend, I was more than happy to play along.

Plus, she sure as shit wasn't gonna stay anywhere Keegan could find her, not if I could help it.

Naw, I'd make sure my little dove felt safe tonight.

"You ready?" I whispered next to her ear, then kissed the top of her head for effect.

But I wasn't sure who I was really fooling with the act: me or the officers.

She nodded, then followed me to my motorcycle.

Standing in the street, I zipped my jacket she still had on, covering her chest, then eased the helmet over her head. Once on the seat, I steadied the bike, then waited for her to climb on behind me.

Without prompting her, she leaned her body against mine, wrapping her arms around me.

"Sal." The shortened version of my name hit my ears.

"Yeah."

"Will you take me home?" Her words came out barely above a whisper. And they sounded more like a plea than a question. "You know, to your place. Please."

To my surprise, she slipped her hands under my shirt, then pressed her warm palms against my abs.

"Yes, Ma'am." I couldn't resist the grin that toyed with my lips. "Anything you want, you just need to ask, *mi pequeña paloma*."

9

Cindy

His words whispered in my mind, *mi pequeña paloma.*

A local Tex-Mex restaurant came to mind, one I'd eaten at with a classmate, Rebecca Franks, on a regular basis over the last five to six years. It had one of the same words in it: *La Paloma Taqueria.*

Does paloma *mean dove?*

I knew what a *taqueria* was, well, somewhat—a place that made tacos. And right now, my brain actually felt too numb to function on any normal level. So, I made a mental note to look up the meaning later once I had charged my phone.

A light fog hung in the surrounding air, creating

a damp mist that coated the side of my face and the clothing covering my body.

"Hold on." Salvador's voice rose over the sound of the engine. "I'm going to cross lanes."

As instructed, I tightened my grip, drawing strength and comfort from the warmth of his body.

He eased across three lanes of the expressway, exited the ramp, then stayed on the access road.

Fat droplets of rain plopped against my pants, permeating the fabric, and they also splattered on the visor of the helmet.

My thoughts turned to Salvador. Twice, I'd dragged him into a false reality with the webs of deceit I had spun. And each time, he had done nothing to dispel the untruths.

For someone who believed in the lawyer's oath, swore to become a guardian of truth and to wield the rule of law as an instrument of justice, I sure had fallen short of that pledge today.

What must he think of me?

The thought made my stomach swirl in a mixed-up sludge of sour fluid that left a burning ache in the pit of my belly.

That I'm a lying bitch, that's what!

In truth, I really wished I could turn off the negative voice in my head. The one telling me I wasn't worth the pound of flesh that kept my insides covered. Since early childhood, all I heard was how I had damaged my mother's womb, preventing her from giving my father the son he yearned for—that he wanted above all else.

Why do you want to be an attorney? My father had asked me when I picked my college major, criminal justice, with every intention of becoming a top-notch lawyer. *You'll never make partner. You're just a breeder.*

His words had hurt me, cut me to the core. All I wanted was to make him proud.

A shudder shook my upper body, and a strangled sob left my lips. Tucking my shielded face against Salvador's back, I squeezed my eyes shut, willing the tears to recede.

He passed a few intersections, then turned left onto a street.

The unfamiliar residential subdivision housed older homes. If guessing, the structures had a good eighty to ninety years on them. Many of them needed some work, but they all had mature trees and loads of character.

Salvador slowed, turned down a winding dead-end street that led to a cul-de-sac, pulled into the double concrete drive of a two-story house, then parked next to his Jeep.

The house, light gray with smoky blue roof shingles and trim, had a wraparound porch.

A couple of ocean blue metal chairs sat on either side of a standard-sized window with a round table holding a marble chess set sandwiched between them. An occupant of one of the chairs, a salt-n-peppered man—with more salt than pepper—smoked a rolled cigarette. Or, at least, I hoped it was a normal one filled with tobacco.

"Climb off." Salvador held the motorcycle steady.

Once I swung my leg over and got off, he deployed the kickstand, then joined me.

The elderly man snuffed out his cigarette on an upright cinderblock next to the love seat, pinched the end of his rolled smoke, then dropped it into his front pocket. Slowly, the man rose, then shuffled to the end of the porch.

"Let me help you." Salvador eased the helmet from my head.

The minute it came off, thoughts of my flat, messy hair came to mind.

I must look a mess.

"Well, now?" Slowly, the elderly man made progress. "Who is your female friend?" He shuffled to the end of the porch.

"Grandpa." Salvador motioned for me to follow him. "This is Cindy. We work together."

"Hi." I held out a hand. "Cindy Stevens. It's nice to meet you, Mr. Vargas."

I had taken a fifty-fifty guess on the surname and hoped I'd gotten the name right.

"Likewise, *Meja*." Mr. Vargas took my hand in his.

The handshake was firm but gentle. He seemed to study my face with an astute eye, then his gaze flicked to Salvador.

"Did you make her cry?" The man's face took on a stern, serious expression.

"No, Sir." Salvador shook his head, but his grandfather turned those intense eyes on me.

"Uhm, no." I shook my head and wasn't sure what to say. "Someone broke into my apartment."

"Are you okay, *Meja*?" Concern flickered in his eyes, and his features softened.

"Yeah." I placed a hand on Salvador's forearm. "I'm just glad that Salvador was with me."

"You were home during the break-in?" asked his grandfather.

"No, Grandpa, she wasn't." Salvador seemed to study the marble chessboard pieces from afar. "It happened when we were at the bar, workin'. I drove her home because someone had slashed her tires in the parking lot at work." He stepped onto the porch.

"You're not going back there tonight, are you?" Mr. Vargas posed the question.

"Well, I, um . . ."

"You'll stay here." Mr. Vargas spoke without hesitation. "Salvador will give up his room."

"No." I shook my head. "I couldn't inconvenience you or him like—"

"Nonsense. It isn't safe at your place." The elderly man turned determined eyes on Salvador. "You will stay. We'll keep you safe, *Meja*."

The genuine glint in the man's eyes spoke volumes in regard to his old-fashioned way. I could've easily rented a hotel room, but then again, I really didn't want to stay somewhere alone.

Rain pelted the grass, sidewalk, street, and driveway. Every few seconds, a gust of wind below droplets onto the porch that hit the back of my body, making my clothing cling to me.

"Thank you." I offered the older man a warm smile.

Salvador stood next to the little table. His hand hovered over the gameboard. He remained silent. His fingers tittered between a few pieces, then hung inches from one of two on the board.

The old man cleared his throat. "Are you sure about that one?"

"I am now." Salvador grabbed the second of the two, then set the piece down.

"Checkmate." The old man chuckled.

"I should've played the other one." A grin split Salvador's full, kissable lips, revealing a single dimple on his right cheek.

"Nope." I shook my head. "You were doomed before you even picked up that piece."

"What?" Salvador's gaze bounced to me.

"One move or seven," I said, placing the pieces onto the board for a new game. "Your grandfather already had the game."

"You can't win them all." Mr. Vargas clasped a hand on Salvador's shoulder, then looked back at me. "Do you play, *Meja*?"

"Yes." I nodded.

A chill settled on my skin, and I shuttered.

"We should play a game sometime, but for now, let's get you two inside and dry." Mr. Vargas turned around, then headed to the front door.

After wiping my feet on the doormat, I stepped over the threshold.

The entrance led to a large open floor plan with a living room directly to the left and a kitchen to the right.

Inside the living room, a worn leather couch and recliner filled a space in front of an entertainment center. Off to the side, near a cornered fireplace, two high-backed wooden chairs with seat cushions sat around a small glass with a chessboard in play.

Without saying a word, Salvador walked over to the board, studied the pieces, then made a move. When he glanced up, his gaze locked with mine, and I couldn't help but grin.

"What?" Salvador approached me.

"Are you even trying?" I whispered. "He's gonna have you in less than six."

"We'll see." Salvador winked, then crossed the open space to the dining area.

A built-in horseshoe bench caught my eye. It covered a bay window with a custom-made wooden table. Another chessboard sat at the end of the wooden surface, and a laugh escaped my lips.

Just like the other two times, Salvador studied the pieces, then made a move. However, unlike the others, this one was anyone's game at this stage.

Hardwood floors ran as far as I could see.

"Care for something hot?" His grandfather stepped into the adjacent kitchen.

"Sure." I slide off Salvador's jacket, draping it over one end of the bench, then studied the chess pieces closely. "That'd be lovely."

"I'll be back. Gonna dry up." Water dripped off Salvador's wet head, and his shirt stuck to his chest and shoulders. "And I'll find you something to wear." He grabbed his jacket, then headed up the stairs to the upper level of the house.

His leather pants drew my attention—well, namely his butt, and I wondered if the leather had protected his lower body from the rain.

"*Meja.*" Mr. Vargas' voice cut through my thoughts. "Do you drink tea or coffee?"

I turned around and held the elderly man's gaze.

An all-knowing smile split his lips.

A warmth spread across my chest, up my neck, and over my face.

Busted. My eyes widened. *Great. Grandpa caught me checking out Sal.*

"Coffee," I managed to squeak out. "Decaf, if you have it. If not, anything will do."

He opened a cabinet, then pulled out a glass container with a green top. "Instant, okay?"

"Yes. Sir." I nodded.

He pressed a button on the kettle against the wall, and the electronic device popped into motion. "So, *Meja*, how long have you and my Salvador been dating?"

"What? We're not . . ."

10

Salvador

"Ya'll make a handsome couple," Grandpa said. "Are you two exclusive?"

And the awkward questions begin . . .

Cindy's eyes grew large and round, like pools of ocean water. It wasn't as if I blamed her.

Hell, about now, I'm sure my expression mirrors hers.

Only difference, after twenty-seven years, I'm used to the things that come out of the man's unfiltered mouth.

"Grandpa. We only work together, remember?" I handed Cindy a pair of my fitted sweatpants and a long-sleeved matching sweatshirt. "It's all I got, but it's dry."

"Thanks." Cindy smiled, drawing my attention to her pink, heart-shaped lips.

Her fingers brushed against mine, and it was as if an electric jolt of energy covered my skin where she had touched me.

She sucked in a quick breath, and a little mew of a sound escaped her lips.

"The downstairs bathroom's under the stairs." I motioned in the general direction.

"Okay, thanks." Cindy darted out of the room as quick as her legs would take her.

What must she think? I exhaled a heavy sigh.

"She is a pretty girl." My grandfather nudged me with an elbow.

"I suppose so."

"*Mejo*. I have eyes, you know? And ears." He pointed at his face, then reached for the kettle. "They both work just fine."

"What's that supposed to mean?" I grabbed the sugar container, then carried it to the table.

"It means what I said. I'm not blind." He chuckled. "I see the chemistry between the two of you."

Soft footsteps drew my attention to the living room.

Seeing her wearing my clothing only high-lighted her smaller frame. Even though the top and pants fit her baggy, there was something about the way she looked in my stuff that I liked.

"Uhm . . ." Cindy entered the kitchen. "I, um, I hung my clothing on a rack in the bathroom to dry. I hope that's okay."

"That's good." I couldn't help but stare at her. "I'll toss them in the wash and dry them for you in a bit."

"If you show me where the washroom is, I can do it."

"Naw." I shook my head.

"You're a guest." A warm smile hit Grandpa's lips. "Come join us. Sit. Sit. " He motioned to the table.

"Okay." She didn't seem her usual, put together self. In fact, she appeared nervous and about to leap out of her skin.

"*Meja*." My grandfather waved to her. "How do you like your coffee?"

"Do you have any milk or half-n-half?" A ruddiness covered her cheeks, giving her face more color than I'd seen all night.

"In the fridge." I motioned with a thumb over my shoulder.

"I'll get it." Cindy made her way into the open kitchen.

She approached the refrigerator door and grabbed the handle.

"Seriously?" Laughter escaped from between her lips.

I glanced at her over my shoulder. "What?"

She opened the door and grabbed the pint-sized carton. Once she had closed the refrigerator, she tapped the stainless-steel surface.

"Do you two have ongoing games all over the house?" A soft giggle rose from her direction.

"We do." Grandpa stood next to her. "Feel free to play. You may go first."

Cindy shot a glance my way, her eyes asking an unspoken question.

"Go for it." I set the sugar on the table. "He's always eager to play new blood. But don't go easy on him."

"Oh, I won't." She held the half-n-half in one hand, reset the magnetic game board with the other, then made her first move. 1.g4—an unconventional one at that—then joined me at the table.

My grandfather approached the refrigerator and clicked his tongue a few times, taking in Cindy's move. She had opened by immediately moving the king knight's pawn two squares ahead.

"Do you know what this attack is called?" My grandfather studied the board for a few more seconds, glanced at Cindy, then his gaze returned to the newly kicked-off game.

"Yes, Sir." Cindy nodded. "The Grob Attack, named after international Master Henri Grob."

"That is correct," my grandfather said, now fully intrigued by the game, as well as in Cindy. "He played hundreds of correspondence games with it. Henri often referred to it as the Spike Opening."

"Well, now you've done it," I whispered to her.

"What?" Confusion flashed across her face.

"You done gone and spoken his language." I headed to the kitchen, grabbed three mugs, then spooned coffee crystals into each of them. "Now, there's no escape."

A quick glance in my grandfather's direction confirmed the man still studied the board, contemplating his next move. After a handful of minutes, he made his move.

Grabbing the mugs, I carried all three to the table.

"It's your move, *Meja*." My grandfather shuffled behind me, then sat.

Cindy glanced at the board, then made her move. "Your go."

A playful grin tugged at my grandfather's mouth, and that quick spark of intelligence I knew all too well gleamed in his eyes. I hadn't seen the man this giddy over a game in ages.

She slipped onto the opposite side of my grandfather, then slide across the bench, making room for me to join her.

He studied her face just as much, if not more, than he scrutinized his next move.

Ring.

Ring.

Ring.

An old-fashioned wall phone, with a curled, springy cord, hung on the wall.

"Well, now." Grandpa rose. "Who'd be callin' at this late hour?"

Once again, the man's feet shuffled across the floor, then he picked up the receiver.

"Howdy, Malcom's Mortuary." Grandpa's voice took on a deep baritone. "You stab 'em, we'll slab 'em." A slight pause for effect followed. "You kill 'em, we'll chill 'em. And if you snuff 'em, we'll stuff 'em."

"He didn't just say that?" Cindy's mouth dropped open.

"You're lucky that's all he said," I whispered. "The man's incorrigible."

She sat close enough that the warmth of her body permeated my clothing.

A light, clean melon and peach scent, with a hint of mint, tickled my nose. It was the perfume she wore—Halston, if guessing.

At work, I could tell when she had entered a room at

the club. And all too often, I'd follow the scent, sniffing her out. The fragrance had become one of my favorite aromas to encounter over the last six weeks or so.

Cindy had become a puzzle for me to decipher. Where others saw an uppity, waspy bitch, I perceived her as an unsolved mystery.

There's more to her than meets the eye.

"Slow down." My grandfather pressed the phone to one ear and covered the other with a cupped hand. "For God's sake, woman, slow down."

"Who is it, Grandpa?"

"You want what?" Grandpa raised his voice. "Money? Time? What? I can't hear you, Carmen. You'll need to talk to *Mejo*."

"I'm not here," I whispered, then made the cutoff motion with my hand to my neck.

"He's right here." He shuffled over to me, then shoved the receiver in my face. "Talk to your *Tia*. She's blabbering about something."

Fuck. Really? She is the last person in the world I want to talk to.

"Hey, *Tia* Carmen." I scrubbed my voice free of the disdain I felt. "How are you?"

"*Aye, Mejo*," she crooned in my ear. "I've been trying to get a hold of you. Calling you—"

"Yeah, I know. I got all of your messages. I've

been really busy at work, then I had to take care of an emergency. A break-in."

"Is everyone okay? What did they steal? Did they steal the urns? I heard where some robbers dumped a man's mother's ashes down the toilet, then pawned the container for money. *Aye*."

Tia Carmen wailed into the phone, forcing me to hold it away from my ear.

"They took *Mami* and the others, then dumped them out, didn't they?" Big sobs hit the line. "I'll light three candles, one for each of them."

"No, *Tia*. All the urns are here and accounted for." I exhaled a long sigh, trying not to let frustration push me over the edge. "So, why did you call?"

"Oh, I need to know who your plus one is, *Mejo*." Pots and pans clanged in the background.

"My plus one? For what?"

"Don't tell me you forgot."

"Forgot what?"

"*¡Ay, Dios!*" She wailed into the phone once more, making my ears ache. "How could you forget the most important day of *Meja*'s life?"

Fuck, I mouthed the word. "I didn't forget, *Tia* Carmen."

"You did," whispered Grandpa, then he looked at Cindy. "He did. He forgot."

"No, I didn't." I narrowed my eyes in warning and motioned for my grandfather to shut the fuck up.

"You did." She sobbed into the phone. "And you're standing in at the wedding. How could you forget?"

"I didn't forget!" My gaze landed on Cindy.

She had an animated look on her face, and to make it worse, she mouthed, *you forgot*.

A thought formed in my head. "*Tia* Carmen, I swear, I didn't forget." I grinned at Cindy. "I'm even bringing someone. A girl."

"A date?" My *Tia's* sobs dried up instantly. "As in a girlfriend? Not just a friend that's a girl, right? A real girl."

"Yeah. Cindy Stevens—she's my girl."

Cindy's mouth dropped open once again. "What?"

"*Tia*, I gotta go. We're visiting with Grandpa." I cracked a grin, then hung up.

Hey, she volunteered me for a party. *I'm just returning the favor.*

"Wait." Her eyebrows had more bounce than an acrobat on a trampoline. "Where are you taking me?"

"To a wedding." I suppressed a chuckle. "So, you can meet all the family."

"But I can't go to that as your—"

"Sure you can." I slid onto the seat next to her, placing my arm on the back of the booth behind her.

"After all, I'm your plus one for your father's firm event." I winked at her. "Turnabout's fair play," I whispered in her ear.

"I knew she was your girl." Grandpa busted out laughing.

11

Cindy

"So, Mr. Vargas." Cindy hid behind her mug. "Tell me something about Salvador that most people don't know."

The need to find out why Salvador would drag me to an actual family event kept me spiraling out of control, making it hard to maintain a cool, calm composure. But with the present company, his grandfather, I didn't want to approach the topic. There'd be time for that once I got Salvador alone.

"Well, do you see that little line on his nose? That scar?" Mr. Vargas pointed an index finger at Salvador.

"Yes, Sir." I nodded.

"Well, when he was three, he ran through the house in his Underoos." His gaze flicked to Salvador. "What were they? Spiderman or Superman?"

"Grandpa, she's not interested in hearing about my childhood underwear."

"Speak for yourself." I gave his chest a playful smack. "I'm all ears."

"Well, he had tied a towel around his neck, pretending it was a cape."

"The ever-present protector, even as a kid, huh?" I took a sip of my coffee, then elbowed him gently.

"His grandma, God rest her sweet soul, called out to him, telling him to stop runnin', but he just kept goin'."

The elderly man's eyes sparkled like warm pools of milk chocolate.

"What happen?" An eagerness to learn more about Salvador as a child intrigued me. After all, the man pretty much kept to himself, so this was a chance to obtain a glimpse into the enigma of who he was at the core.

"Instead of listenin' to his grandma, he kept right on runnin'. Seconds later, the ping of broken glass smashing sounded, followed by a crash to the floor."

A gasp left my lips, and I covered my mouth with a hand. "What happened?"

"He'd hit the window in the living room full-speed ahead," his grandfather said. "Smashed right through it."

"Oh, my God!" I turned to face Salvador, only to find he now wore an expressionless mask. "You cut your face on broken glass." My fingers traced the line over the bridge of his nose.

"Yeah." He nodded. "It wasn't a big deal."

"Wasn't a big deal, seriously?" I asked, looking for evidence of other scarring.

His grandfather rose, and shuffled to the kitchen, rinsed his cup, then set it in the sink. "He had a sliver of glass stickin' out his nose almost eight inches long." Mr. Vargas measured with his hands.

"I don't see any stitches." Leaning in closer, I studied his face. "Not a single one."

"That's because there weren't any." Salvador cupped my hand in his.

"What? Why not?"

The skin-on-skin contact made me suck in a sharp breath, then goose bumps erupted up one arm and down the other.

"The ER doctor on call used Superglue and sealed it up nice and tidy like." The elderly man shuffled to the opening of the living room. "Tell her what you were chasing."

"It doesn't matter, Grandpa," he said. "It was a long time ago."

"So, then, it shouldn't matter if you tell me, right?"

"Why do you want to know?" His gaze locked on mine, holding me in place.

The tip of his tongue slid across his lips, drawing my attention to his mouth, making me wonder what he'd feel like, taste like.

Would his lips have a smooth velvety texture to them, or would they be firm and demanding?

"Because I want to know."

"A fly." His response came out as a soft, throaty whisper.

Laughter erupted from my lips. "A fly? You were seriously chasing a fly?"

"Yep." His gaze dropped to my mouth.

A nervous tic from my childhood resurfaced, making my lower lip twitch, and I bit down on it to stop the movement.

Salvador cupped my chin. His thumb brushed over my mouth, freeing my lip, then he leaned in, closing half the distance between his lips and mine.

Inch-by-inch, I found myself migrating toward him, pulled by the invisible strings of attraction.

"You kids don't stay up too late now, ya hear?"

The older man's words ripped me out of the trance I had found myself in.

"We won't, Grandpa." Salvador's gaze returned full force in my direction.

Mr. Vargas' feet shuffled away from the living room and down a dimly lit hallway.

"Now, where were we?" The way Salvador looked at me made me feel seen, really seen, not just viewed on the surface.

His dark chocolate eyes had a way of peering at me as if he gazed deep into my soul, viewing me from the inside out.

"Want to watch a movie?" He slid off the cushion of the bench, then rose.

"Um, sure. Why not?" I scooted off the seat, reached for the mugs, then carried them into the kitchen. "Do you want more coffee?"

"Naw, I'm good." He shook his head, grabbed the sugar, then followed me to the sink.

"What do you like?" I stood next to him, rinsing the mugs. As I finished each one, he took them from me, placing them in the dishwasher.

"Care to be more specific?" His arm rubbed against mine.

Glancing at him, I found him staring again with a single brow arched.

"Movie." The word squeaked free of my mouth.

"Oh." He chuckled. "You want to know what I like to watch?"

A playful glint flashed in his eyes. One I hadn't noticed before.

"Um, yeah."

"Doesn't matter to me. You pick." He put a detergent pouch in the dishwasher, but he didn't turn it on. "How about some popcorn?"

"Does it have extra butter?"

"Not sure." He opened a pantry and extracted a bag. "Just say's it's movie theater butter. Is that okay? If not, I'm sure there's a bag of kernels here somewhere."

"No. That's fine." I examined the buttons on the dishwasher. "Quick wash or normal?"

"What?" He placed the bag in the microwave.

"The cycle." I pointed to the controls. "Which one do you use to wash dishes?"

"Normal," he replied. "But don't start it until the microwave's done."

"Why not?"

"Because it'll knock out the wall, and I'll have to go out to the garage."

"What? Why the garage?"

"To reset the breaker."

Confusion tugged at my brain.

"It's an old house. So, the breakers can't handle more than one appliance running at a time."

When the microwave dinged, he pulled the bag out, then emptied it into a single metal mixing bowl.

"Come on." Salvador pressed start on the dishwasher. Then he placed a hand on my lower back, guiding me out of the kitchen. "Let's see what's on."

The warmth of his hand on me made my stomach flip-flop.

I chanced a quick glance his way, only to find his dark, unreadable eyes trained on me. His gaze pierced my soul as if searching for answers I'd kept hidden for years. He had a way of making me feel seen, of stripping me down to the core of who I was, and, at the moment, I struggled with exactly who that really was.

My father wanted me to marry an up-and-coming prominent man, to bind myself to someone in a loveless marriage. A someone of his choosing, Keegan Black.

The thought of his name made the juices in my stomach sour.

Love's only an illusion, my father had said, *and the sooner you figure that out, the better.*

12

Salvador

An audible ding from her phone cut through the sexual tension in the room, making Cindy jump.

The old 1931 black and white "Dracula" movie playing—a classic favorite of mine—did little to keep my attention. My mind stayed on one topic, one lovely topic, *mi pequeña paloma.*

Hmm. Who's messaging with you, beautiful? The words sat unspoken on the tip of my tongue.

Another buzz hit her phone. She shot a quick glance at it, and her nose scrunched a bit, then she rubbed her eyes. A soft little huff left her lips.

"Are you okay?"

"Yeah, I'm all right. Just a little tired is all."

I grabbed another handful of popcorn out of the bowl, and my fingers collided with hers.

"Sorry." She snapped her hand out of the way. Well, it was more like she flinched.

"No, go ahead." I winked at her. "I've had more than my fair share of it. Plus, we can make more if needed."

"Are you sure?" She seemed hesitant to follow through, even though I could see she wanted to.

The fact she had flinched from my touch unnerved the fuck out of me.

Damn. I'd never hurt her.

"Positive." I brought the arm I'd draped over the back of the couch closer, so that my hand rested just above her shoulder.

Her reluctance to help herself to more popcorn only fueled my anger toward her ex-boyfriend, Keegan.

That fucker needs to learn a lesson on manners—not to mention how to treat a girl.

When she didn't move to scoop up more, I grabbed a single, fluffy popped kernel.

"Here." I offered her the piece, wondering if she would take it from my fingers.

The tip of her pink little tongue darted out, brushing the top of her lower lip. She swallowed hard. Then just when I thought she'd turn away, her lips parted, and she meet me halfway.

A grin split my lips, and I eased the white fluffy popped kernel between her lips.

Damn. The creamy, soft touch of her lips made the head of dick throb.

Without tearing my gaze from hers, I dropped a couple of pieces of popcorn into my mouth.

"Want more?" I offered her access to the bowl once more. But hell, I was more than happy to feed her if that's what she wanted or needed.

She nodded, then grabbed a few pieces. The smile on her pink lips lit up her face.

Once again, her phone dinged, then seconds later, a call hit the device. She glanced at the screen, then her gaze returned to the scene unfolding on the television.

"Do you need to answer that?"

"Uhm, no." She shook her head, sending her hair back and forth to brush against my arm.

"You sure about that?"

"Yeah. It's only my father."

"He might be worried about you. You know, with what happened earlier."

"Me, no." Again, she shook her head, but this time, pain dimmed the light in her eyes. "He's only worried about the name—his reputation."

"What?" Her words confused me. "I don't get it. What do you mean by his reputation?"

"He's upset about the police."

"Well, of course he's upset." My hand cupped her shoulder, drawing her closer to my side. "Someone broke into your place."

Keegan and his fucking friends trashed it. The thought came crashing down in my mind.

"You don't get it." A small huff left her pursed lips.

"Then help out," I said. "Tell me how it is."

"My father, he, uhm, he doesn't like bad publicity."

"Most people don't, but I fail to see how that has anything to do with reporting a crime."

"The fact that there's even a report at all, that's what he'll care about."

"What should that even matter? You didn't do anything wrong. Keegan did."

"Exactly. The law firm isn't called Stevens, Black, & Tillman for nothing." Her gaze darted to mine. "Keegan's father, Randall Black, is one of his partners."

"Good to know." The lines of her irises pulled me in for a closer view. In the center of her eye, a starburst of golden flecks surrounded her pupils. Something I hadn't noticed before. "But you don't work there . . ."

"No, I don't."

"Why not?"

"Because my father doesn't believe women belong in the field of law, or any industry outside of teaching, nursing, or mothering. The man's a pig. He'd rather I marry someone of his choosing."

"Let me guess. Someone like Keegan?"

"Yeah. But that's not gonna happen."

Damn straight. The words surfaced in my brain. *Not if I have anything to do with it.*

I'm left to wonder where the fuck that thought came from.

"Hey, you have one life to live. So, live it the way you want, not the way others dictate."

She grew silent and chewed on her lower lip for several seconds, as if contemplating my words.

"Enough about me. What's up with you and your aunt?"

She had chosen to ease into a different topic, which, for now, I'd allow. But at some point, she'd need to revisit the current subject because it was the big-ass fucking elephant dancing and prancing in the room.

"Nothing." I shook my head.

"Didn't seem like nothing."

"My aunt, well, let's just say she's not happy unless she's knee-deep in everyone else's business."

"And that means what?"

"That's she's always busting my balls." A chuckle left my lips. "She thinks it's high-time I found a girl and introduced her to the family. *Tia Carmen's* relentless. Trust me, you don't want on the receiving end of her virtual matchmaker going-ons."

"Hence the plus one comment."

"Exactly."

"Well, if it makes you feel any better . . ." she whispered in my ear. "We can be each other's plus one at events to keep family off our backs. What do ya say?"

"Me." The grin on my lips grew wider, and I winked at her. "You got yourself a date."

"No, both of us have a date—a plus one date." Her soft giggle met my ears, and her eyes lit up like sparkling sapphires.

Bam.

Bam.

Bam.

The three rapid knocks on the door made her jump. Her body grew stiff, and she sprung from the sofa.

"Open up, you fucker," shouted Javier from the other side of the door.

Whines, yips, and playful growls met my ears, and I let out a deep sigh.

"Is t-that, Javier?" Color had drained from Cindy's face, and she plopped back on top of the couch. "What's he d-doing here?"

"Dropping off the love birds' children." Reluctantly, I rose, then headed for the door.

"What? Whose children?" Cindy scooted to the edge of the cushion but remained seated. "What are you talking about?"

"Augustin's and Isa's dogs." I shot a glance over my shoulder. "They asked me and Grandpa to watch them since they're hiding out at the hotel. Didn't want to leave them alone at the house."

"Oh." She chewed on her lower lip, drawing my attention to her mouth.

Blindly, I felt for the deadbolt, unlocked it, swung the door open, then stepped to the side.

"About time, fucker." Javier held two dog leashes, one wrapped around each wrist.

Estrello, Isa's Calupoh Mexican Wolfdog, bounced across the threshold, neck and neck with Zeus, the black lab belonging to Augustin Méndez. The furry duo dragged Javier to the couch to say hello to Cindy.

"Hey," I raised my voice. "Outside."

Zeus reached her first, climbing onto her lap. A surprised shriek left Cindy's lips, followed by high-pitched laughter.

"You're such a sweet boy, aren't you?" She wrapped her arms around Zeus' neck, then showered him with hugs, pats, and scratches.

Estrello wormed his way onto the couch, then rolled over for a tummy rub, which Cindy was all too happy to dish out.

A grin hit my lips. I wasn't sure who enjoyed the contact more: Cindy or the dogs she showered with attention. Honestly, the fur-faces ate that shit up.

13

Cindy

"Whatcha doing?" Javier eyed Salvador. His gaze flicked to me, then back to Salvador.

"What's it look like I'm doin'?" asked Salvador. "We're watchin' a movie."

"Dracula." Curling my legs under me, I wedged my toes between the cushion I sat on and the one next to me. "Want to join us?" I held the bowl up. "We can make more popcorn."

"What the fuck's wrong with the screen?" Javier pointed. "The fuckin' tube go out?"

"Naw, man. It's the 1931 showing of *Dracula*." Salvador shook his head. "What?" He sat in the middle of the couch next to me. "You've never seen an old movie before? A black-n-white?"

"Not one without color." He stifled a yawn. "Except for The Wizard of OZ, but that only had some of the parts in color, not all of it."

"Oh, I love that movie." When I leaned back, my neck brushed against the back of Salvador's arm.

"Well, that shit's old-school." Javier laughed, then his focus flicked to the couch, namely the way his friend and I now sat. "What's with the wolfman behind bars?"

"Part of the show, man," said Salvador.

At this point, I wasn't sure if he was going to move his arm now because of the house guest. A part of me hoped he wouldn't, but another part struggled with the fear that he would.

Did I want him to put this arm around me?

He had treated me with nothing but the utmost respect today, even offered me a shoulder of comfort back at my place. And earlier at the club, he had come to my defense, something I wasn't accustomed to.

But what if he's like Keegan?

The thought sent a chill racing up my spine that made me shiver.

What if all men were like my ex, and well, my father?

"Hey, you cold?" He didn't even wait for me to

answer. Instead, Salvador wrapped a blanket around me.

"Thanks." The word came out as soft as a whisper.

"You stayin' or what?" Salvador propped his feet on the coffee table.

"Not sure." Javier shrugged his shoulders. "Depends on what my girl's doing. And speakin' of the devil..."

Javier stared at the screen of his phone for several seconds, then two-thumbed a message. A grin spread across his lips, making me think of the hookah-smoking character, 'The Caterpillar,' from the beloved classic tale, *Alice in Wonderland*.

"Hey." Javier glanced up from his phone. "Gotta run. The ball-n-chain needs milk and diapers for the kid."

"Wait." His words had stunned me. "You have a child?"

"Naw, not me. It's not mine." He shook his head. "It's her kid."

"But you provide for them both?"

"Sure, why not?" Javier headed to the front door. "She's my girl."

"So, does she have a boy or a girl?" I was still trying to digest the fact that he didn't balk at taking care of another man's child. "And how old is the child?"

"A boy, Lucas." Javier opened the door. "He's under a year. Still drinks formula, the expensive kind."

"If she had breastfed, it wouldn't cost a dime. Be better for the brain development too." The words came out unfiltered.

"Yeah, you tell her that." He stepped outside, chuckling.

"Sorry. I shouldn't have said that." I fidgeted with the last few partially popped kernels in the bowl. "It's n-none of my business."

Salvador approached the door. "Am I picking you up in the morning?" He kept his voice low and calm. "Or are you catching a ride with Clemente to the bar?"

"Clem's givin' me a ride." Javier slipped the phone in his front pocket.

"Don't be late." The ring of authority in Salvador's voice held a chill to it, one I hadn't heard before.

"What about her?" Javier nodded toward me.

"What about her?" Salvador stood motionless just inside the doorframe.

"She stayin' here tonight? Tomorrow?"

"Yeah," replied Salvador. "At least until it's safe for her to return to her place."

I rose and covered half the distance to the door, clutching the popcorn bowl in my hands.

"I, uhm, I can go with you to the bar tomorrow." Suddenly, it felt as if I had overstepped my welcome. "Mina wants a full inventory of the beverages so I could start it in the morning. That way, I'm not imposing on you and your grandfather."

"I'll see you at six sharp, you and Clemente," Salvador said to Javier as more of a command than a statement.

"You know what? I just remember, I have this thing." I pulled the Uber app on my screen. "I should go and—"

"You're not going anywhere." He closed the door, then turned to face me.

"But I need to—"

"What you need to do is sit, watch the rest of the movie, and relax." He closed the gap between his body and mine in only a couple of strides. "You're under my protection. So, whatever you need to do, you can do it from here."

"I don't want to impose on you and your—"

"You're not imposing, Cindy." His hand wrapped around my bicep, sending a wave of heat to travel throughout my body. "Besides, my grandpa likes you, and he'd skin me alive if I let you leave the house at this hour. Okay?"

I nodded, then said, "Yeah."

"How long do you think it will take you to do inventory?" he asked. "And will you need some muscle to move things around?"

"No." He stood so close, I could smell the hints of vanilla and musk in his cologne. "I can manage."

"Are the kegs and boxed liquor bottles in the back part of the inventory?"

"Yes." My phone buzzed in my pocket on silent mode. "She wants a full count."

"Then I'll have some extra guys there to help."

"You don't have to do that."

He drew me into his arms. "I know. But I want to."

Once again, my phone buzzed in my pocket, and when I didn't answer it, a FaceTime call rang through, making me jump.

"You gonna get that?"

I shook my head.

"Why not?" He held my gaze. "Might be important."

Once again, I shook my head. After all, I could count the people on one hand who called me on FaceTime: my mother, my uncle, Keegan, and my father when angry with me. And if my suspicions were correct, I'd see my father's angry face on the screen.

Salvador slid one hand around my waist, drawing me closer to his lean frame, then with his other, he extracted the phone from my back pocket.

"Wait. You can't . . ."

I reached for my cell, but he held it just out of reach.

"Hello," he said.

"Your father is—wait, who are you?" My mother's voice rose from the phone. "Where's Cindy? Is she okay? Was she hurt?"

"Mom, I'm fine." I reached for the phone once more, but Salvador kept a tight hold on it.

"Are you safe?" my mother asked. "Where are you?"

"Yes. I'm safe," I replied. "I'm staying with a friend."

"What friend?" Curiosity coated my mother's words. "Who was that boy?"

"Name's Salvador," he said, then relinquished control of the phone.

14

Salvador

"Mom, wait. I'm . . ." She removed the call from speaker. "No. I'm fine. Safe." A brief pause passed. "No. I'm staying with my friend . . . his grandfather's place . . . no, Mom. Don't put Dad on. I don't want to—"

Cindy made her way to the bathroom, stepped inside, then closed the door.

Her reaction to her mother, and not wanting to speak to her father, had garnered my full attention. It was the first time I'd caught a glimpse of the odd dynamics of her family in action.

Standing on the other side of the door, I watched the light under the door shift each time she paced.

What started out as hushed whispers grew in volume. And her father's voice rose the highest.

"Give me the address, now," demanded her father.

"I don't know it," her voice quivered, "and I don't need to—"

"I'll take care of your apartment and the police report. Now, turn on the tracking app like a good girl." Once again, her father gave her a direct order. "I've already talked to Keegan. He *will* pick you up."

"No!" Panic coated her words. "How could you even suggest that he . . . after what he's done to me . . . what he did to my place—"

"All couples have disagreements."

"A disagreement, really? Oh, come on, Dad, you can do better than that. Couples engage in scrimmages all the time that involve what toothpaste to buy, where to eat out, or what side of the bed to sleep on. But what happened tonight—what's been happening the past year—isn't as simplistic as a disagreement. Keegan slashed my tired, trashed my apartment, killed my pets, and he physically hurt—"

"Stop being melodramatic. You and Keegan will kiss and make up."

Silence met her father's words.

"You're no longer a kid in college, Cindy. So, it's

time to grow up and do as I say. Do you understand?"

"Oh, I understand exactly what you're saying. But hear this, I'll never get back together with him. Never."

"Yes. You. Will. You will do what I tell you to do because it's what's best for the family. Or I'll cut you off."

"Fine. Go ahead. Do it! I don't need your money," she scoffed. "I have a job—a means to support myself. I'm not helpless. And I don't need your financial assistance, and I sure don't need or want Keegan's."

"Give me the fucking address!"

"No," her response was little more than a whisper.

A slow-burning fury simmered under the breaking point of my resolve.

I wasn't about to let *mi pequeña paloma* out of my sight. I didn't give a fuck who asked, pleaded, or begged. She wasn't leaving my side tonight. And tomorrow, I'd assign some men to watch over her. No one, not Keegan or his crew, or even her fucking father, would come anywhere near her, not if I had anything to say or do about it.

Silence filled the space for several seconds, then running water sounded.

Only one issue stood between *mi paloma* and myself. *Will she let me in to her world—accept my help?* Would she confide in me?

Now that the call was over, I'd back off and give her some privacy. Let her compose herself. So, I made my way to the living room, grabbed her cup, then headed to the kitchen to refresh her drink.

A scratch at the backdoor grabbed my attention.

Plastered against the glass panes of the French doors were two sets of eyes, four fur-faced lips, and two overly wet tongues.

Damn, how'd I get babysitting duty?

My gaze flicks to the instant decaf coffee, then to the Sleepy Time mint tea box.

Maybe something soothing to drink will help.

Mind made up, I pressed the lever on the kettle, then approached the door. Hand on the knob, I twisted it.

The moment the door opened, Zeus and *Estrello* both shot through the door, their nails tapping against the kitchen tile.

"Hey," I raised my voice. "Slow down."

The dynamic duo trotted into the living room. Seconds later, little whines, playful growls, and yips met my ears.

"Salvador?" Cindy's voice grabbed my attention.

The kettle dinged, indicating it had reached one-hundred-and-eighty degrees.

"In here." I rinsed her cup and mine, grabbed two of the individual tea bags, then put one inside of each mug.

Tea kettle in hand, I poured the water over each bag, returned the pot to its resting spot, then reached for some agave nectar.

"Mmm." Cindy stepped into the kitchen.

A dog flanked her on each side, their tails wagging in tandem with one another.

"Something smells good." She drew in a deep breath. "Is that some kind of mint tea? Chamomile or lemongrass?"

I picked up the box and scanned the ingredients.

"Yes. All the above." My gaze flicked to hers, and she glanced away as if to avoid looking at me. "Says here, it has chamomile, spearmint, lemongrass, tilia flowers—whatever those are—blackberry leaves, orange blossoms, hawthorn, and rosebuds."

"Well, it smells divine."

"I see you have attracted a couple of shadows."

"Guess so." One of her shy smiles touched her lips, and she shot a quick glance my way, but seconds later, diverted her red, blood-shot eyes.

"You okay?" My question made her fidget, and I

knew full well she wasn't okay, not after that fuckin' call she had with her bastard-of-a-father.

What man tosses his blood into a shitstorm like that?

My hands closed into tight fists.

"I'm good."

"You sure? Cuz it looks like you've been crying." And with that comment, playing it cool and waiting for her to come to me with the conversation went out the window. "Want to talk about it?"

"Oh, this?" She gestured to her eyes. "I've just had my contacts in too long. Plus, allergies have been killing me as of late." Her plastic, well-rehearsed smile surfaced. "I'm fine. Honestly. It's nothing."

I'd give her a short reprieve for now, but at some point, she and I would really need to talk about the growing fucking elephant in the pink tutu dancing in the room. But, again, for now, I'd back the fuck off because I didn't want her to shut down.

"Come on, let's sit." I handed her the teacup, then brushed past her, heading for the living room. "Besides, we've only seen half the movie. The best parts are comin' up."

Gesturing to the sofa, I give her the choice of where to sit.

Back on the couch, she curled up on one end of the couch. Zeus circled around her feet then snuggled into a ball on the floor next to her legs. But

Estrello, the cockblocker he was, plopped on the middle cushion with his head on her lap.

"Hey, move it." I motioned to him, but he only groaned. "Off."

Estrello, all stretched out and taking up two-thirds of the sofa, flashed me a defiant gaze.

Grabbing his collar, I guided him off, then sat next to Cindy. Seconds later, the little cock blocker wormed his way back onto the couch, trying to drive a wedge between his body and mine, as if to keep me away from the only female in the house.

"Hey." I reached for the dog. "What did I tell you?"

"Aww." Laughter left her lips. "Someone just wants some lovin' . . . don't ya?"

He rolled onto his back, exposing his belly.

"Okay. Okay." She giggled some more. "A belly rub it is."

You sneaky cock-blocking little fucker.

15

Cindy

"No one plays Drac like Béla Lugosi." I took a sip of tea, relishing the smoothness of it going down.

"You think?"

"Yep." My hand blindly found the inside of the popcorn bowl. "I know it." I chased some of the fluffy popped kernels around. "It's one of his better roles, if not his best."

"Naw." He shook his head, then pulled the popcorn away. "Take that back."

"What?" His gesture took me by surprise. Even *Estrello*, now wedged between me and the corner of the couch, glanced up—his ears stood up, and his eye remained alert.

"What you said, take it back." His lips parted into a playful grin.

"He made a better Drac—"

"Uh-uh." He shook his head. "Hands down, he made a better Frankenstein monster than Dracula! But if you're talking, Drac, Boris Karloff is the man!"

"That's blasphemy." I tossed a piece of popcorn at him, and he caught it with his mouth.

"Naw, *mi pequeña paloma,* there's nothing sacrilegious about it. And just to prove it . . ." He grabbed his phone. "I'm gonna call my *Tia* to ask. She loves the classics."

"You are not." Reaching across him, I took a dive for his phone, straddling him in the process.

Laughter bubbled inside of me, then exploded from my lip. I hadn't felt this carefree, this unburdened in. Well, I couldn't recall the last time.

"Don't think I won't." He held his phone just out of reach.

Zeus rose and started barking, then *Estrello* joined in.

"Oh, God. I'm sorry." My eyes widened, and my breath caught in the back of my throat. "Shhh." I motioned to the dogs. "No. No. No. It's okay. Don't bark. You'll wake up—"

"It's okay." Salvador wrapped an arm around my waist, drawing me to his chest.

"No, the dogs." My heart hammered in my chest. "They're going to wake your grandfather."

Thoughts of my paternal grandfather came to mind. The times I spent at his home during summer, winter, and spring breaks flooded my mind and all but choked me. My eyes watered, then tears spilled over the brim of my lids.

"Hey." He wiped tears from my face. "It's okay. With his hearing aids off and his CPAC machine going, the man could sleep through a tornado."

Salvador held my body in place with one arm wrapped around me, and with the other, he caressed the side of my face. His tongue swiped across his lips. Drawn to the motion, I fixated on his mouth. With his arm, he guided me closer, but right before my lips touched his, he stopped.

"Tell me what you want."

"I uhm . . ." My heart thumped in my chest. "I want . . ."

"Tell me."

"I want you to kiss me." The heat of embarrassment hit my face, and I turned from him.

Oh, God, what must he think of me?

"I'm sorry." I squirmed in his arms. "I don't know what came over—"

"Still yourself." He cupped my face, then tipped my chin until my eyes met his.

The tender touch of his lips on mine took my breath away. He showed both restraint and control, allowing me to set the pace, something I'd never experienced before. Keegan had always taken what he wanted when and how he wanted it. But Salvador followed my lead, only taking what I offered.

He opened to me, and I tentatively explored the inside of his mouth. The moment his tongue touched mine, a soft moan expelled from deep within my throat, and I clang to his shirt.

Inching closer to him only pressed his growing erection between my legs, making me well aware of how intimately his body now pressed against mine.

The thought of wanting him, desiring to be with him, was new territory. And if I was reading his reaction right, he wanted me as well.

A low-pitched howl broke the intimate spell and made me jump.

In unison, Salvador and I turned to face *Estrello*, who sat at the other end of the couch.

"Hey, cut that out." Salvador stared at the dog a moment, bowed his head, then claimed my lips again.

Once more, that low-pitched howl emanated from the corner of the couch.

"Seriously?" Salvador sighed, then pressed his forehead to mine.

Estrello sprung from the couch, ran in circles a few times, then ran into the kitchen. Once just inside the open archway, he whined, then howled again.

"What, you want out now?" Salvador sighed again.

The dog responded with another howl, but only this time, Zeus joined him in the kitchen.

"You got some lousy timing there, *Estrello*." Salvador chuckled. "You too, Zeus."

An awkwardness came over me, and when I tried to slide off his lap, I only managed to grind against his erection. I froze in place for a few seconds, then when I finally moved once more, I bump my forehead against Salvador's chin.

"Oh, God, I'm sorry. I uhm . . ."

"Let me help you, *mi pequeña paloma*." A smile split his lips, then he chuckled.

He rose, bringing me with him.

A yelp left my lips, and he chuckled once more.

Once my feet hit the floor, he held me in his arms as if making sure I had my footing.

"Sal." I looked at him.

"Yeah." His chocolaty eyes held the glow of desire, which brought a new round of heat to my face, making me blush.

"What does that mean, what you said? What you called me?"

"*Mi pequeña paloma?*"

"Yes. That."

"My little dove." He tucked a strand of hair behind my ear. "It's an endearment."

"Oh, okay."

"Do you not like it?"

"No." I shook my head, then felt a new wave of heat on my face. "I mean yes, I like it. I don't mind you calling me that."

If being honest with myself, I liked it. I liked it a lot.

"Good." He placed a chaste kiss to my lips, then held my gaze.

Estrello whined, then howled at the back door.

"All right already." He sighed, then released me. "How about I let them out and you make more popcorn?"

"Deal."

He cupped my face and kissed me. "I'll be back, and we can pick up where we left off before someone so rudely interrupted."

Estrello voiced a growl of a complaint, then pawed at the air.

A giggle bubbled on my lips. "I'll be waiting."

I trailed behind him, watching him open the French doors. Once he and the dogs had stepped outside, he closed the door.

Grabbing another bag of popcorn from the pantry, I removed the wrapper, placed it inside the microwave, keyed in the time, then hit start.

Knock.

Knock.

Knock.

A grin hit my lips. I headed to the front door, unlocked it, and then swung it open.

"I didn't think you'd come back." The laughter on the tip of my tongue died. "What are you doing here, Keegan?"

"I could ask you the same thing." He took hold of my wrist and yanked me out of the house.

16

Salvador

Estrello pranced around the yard as if looking for the optimal place to take a fuckin' piss. And each time he stopped, he only squirted a bit of pee, marking the area.

"Hurry up." I leaned against the patio frame. "Do your thing and finish."

Zeus had zipped out into the yard, emptied his bladder, then returned in less than two minutes flat and now waited by the door. But man, the other one, he was takin' his sweet time.

"Hey," I called out to him, and he glanced up with what I swear was a shit-eating-grin. "Yeah, I'm talkin' to you, you little cockblocker."

A whine, followed by an insistent bark, told me Zeus wanted back inside the house.

"I'm not the one holding things up," I said to Zeus. "Tell your mark-happy-buddy over there to shake it off already."

Estrello froze in the middle of the yard. His ears came to stiff points, and the hair on his back and hunches rose. He bared his teeth, and a low, throaty growl met my ears.

Behind me, Zeus scratched at the door, then he too joined in on the growl fest.

Estrello raced across the yard, flew across the patio, then rammed into the glass door.

"What the fuck?" the words left my mouth in a whisper.

A blood-curdling scream pierced the night, sending a cold chill over my skin.

Cindy. Her name bounced in my head with urgency.

The moment I opened the door, both Zeus and *Estrello* raced inside, ushering low, throaty growls.

I stepped over the threshold, leaving the door ajar, then followed the four-legged beasts running through my house.

Another scream sounded, but instead of coming from inside, it sounded distant.

"Cindy," I shouted her name.

I entered the living room just in time to see both of the dogs running out the front door.

Why the fuck is the door open?

Once again, I shouted, "Cindy!"

Outside, in the middle of the front yard, I found Keegan dragging her through the grass.

"Let go." She tugged against his pull.

I was out the front door behind the dogs. Sheer adrenaline fueled my anger. If anyone deserved a beat down, it was that *gringo* piece of shit.

"Stop your shit!" He grasped the neck of the sweatshirt. "Don't make me hurt you."

Cindy wiggled out of the garment. Wearing sweatpants and nothing but a bra on top, she sprung to her feet. She took two steps, then Keegan tackled her, slamming her to the ground.

"*¡Híjole! Este cabrón.*" Blood pumped in my ears, drowning out the surrounding sounds. "Hey, *pendejo.* Let her go."

A shadow stretched across the yard, coming from the street, and a light mist hung in the air. Glancing up, two of Keegan's friends—Kyle Lubbock and Benjamin Reid—rushed forward.

"Where the fuck do you think you're goin'? Huh?" Benjamin came at me in the low, defensive tackle, no doubt, a move he'd learned in football.

The fucker was big, but Benjamin sure as shit

wasn't fast, and his shit-for-brains partner, Kyle, held a goddamn bat in his hands.

"Let me at the Mexican." Kyle gripped the bat with both hands. "I'll get 'em."

Spinning out of the way, I avoid a takedown blow by Benjamin, but walked right into Kyle, swinging the bat.

The first blow missed me, but the second caught my right bicep and a couple of ribs. Before I could recover, what felt like a brick wall—Benjamin—slammed me to the ground, knocking the wind from my lungs.

Cindy's high-pitched screams filled the darkness of the night. A quick glance her way confirmed the fucker had dragged her to the curb, not far from a vehicle.

Zeus latched onto Kyle's arm. He dragged him to the ground, making Kyle scream like a little bitch. And a well-placed knee to Benjamin's groin, had the fucker gasped for air. Once standing, I closed the gap between Keegan and me.

More screams filled the night, and it took a moment for me to realize some of the high-pitched yelps came from Keegan.

The dense mist grew heavy, and then the night sky opened. Rain poured like a shower on full blast, making it hard to see.

Focusing in front of me, I made out a shape.

Estrello had a hold of Keegan's lower leg and, from the way it looked, the furry black beast wasn't gonna let go anytime soon. Taking advantage of the distraction, I rammed into Keegan. The blow took him down to the ground and Cindy with him.

A thud sounded behind me, followed by a yelp. Seconds later, another thud resonated. Making me wonder if Kyle had struck Zeus. Unable to divide my focus, I couldn't turn around to render assistance.

"Call off your friends." My fist made contact with Keegan's face once, twice, thrice, and then I lost count.

The boom of a shotgun blast rung in my ears, freezing me in place.

"You boys get out here," shouted Grandpa. "Or the next ones gonna cost ya a limb or two or your balls."

Cindy crawled away from Keegan, heading toward the house.

Rising, I took one last swing at Keegan, then backed away to help *mi pequeña paloma*.

"I suggest you get goin' now." Grandpa held the weapon on Keegan. "Before I change my mind and fill you boys full of lead."

"Do you know who I am?" Keegan rose with the help of Benjamin.

"I don't rightly care who you are, Son," said Grandpa. "I just care that ya get off my property."

"You made a mistake man, a big fuckin' mistake," Keegan said to me, then his gaze flicked to my grandfather. "Both of you did. I'll see you both in jail for this."

"For what? Protecting what's mine?" asked Grandpa. "You came on my property, threatened my household."

"This isn't over." Keegan's seething gaze bore into me. "You and me . . ."

Zeus limped to the front door, but Estrello held his ground, using his body as a barrier in front of Cindy.

Several tense moments ticked by, then Keegan, Benjamin, and Kyle got into their vehicles and left.

"You okay?" Kneeling, I checked on Cindy.

"I think so." Her body shook.

Extending a hand, I pulled her to her feet, then wrapped my good arm around her shoulders.

"Let's get you two inside and cleaned up," said Grandpa, weapon still in hand. He whistled to the dogs. "Inside, Zeus . . . *Estrello.*"

A few porch lights on the street had turned on, and the movement of curtains inside some of the homes let me know that some of the neighbors had seen the disturbance, making me wonder if anyone had called the police.

If they had, we'd know soon enough.

One thought came to mind . . .

Payback's a bitch! And I intend to unleash her as soon as I know Cindy's safe.

17

Cindy

"Take a seat." Salvador guided me to the couch, then gestured for me to take a seat.

He grabbed his phone from his pocket and two-thumbed a text. Less than ten seconds later, he slipped his phone back into the front of his wet, grass-stained pants.

Zeus limped across the living room, Estrello right behind him.

"Come here, boy," Salvador's grandfather called to Zeus, and the dog waddled up to him. With a gentle touch, he examined first Zeus, then *Estrello*, who whined. "What are you crying about? You're not even hurt." His gaze flicked to Zeus. "And you, you're gonna be just fine with a bit of rest."

What have I done? How had Keegan and his friends found me?

"I'm sorry." I struggled to hold back the tears.

"For what?" Salvador's gaze locked onto mine.

"For all this." I chewed on my lower lip to still the quiver. "None of this would've happened if it wasn't for me."

"Hey." He kneeled in front of me. "This isn't your fault."

"Nope," said his grandfather. "This is all on those boys. We should call the police, get ahead of the situation."

"No." I shook my head. "Please, you can't do that."

"Why's that?" asked Salvador's grandfather.

Because my father will go ballistic, that's why.

A wave of nausea rolled through my stomach, forcing me to breathe through my nose.

"I shouldn't have come here. It was stupid." My knees bounced up and down. "I put you and your grandfather in danger."

"What?" asked Salvador.

"If I wasn't here, they wouldn't have—"

"Naw, you're where ya need to be." He placed his hands on my knees, calming the movement. "You're safe here."

"Damn straight she is," his grandfather said.

"Please, don't call the police," I pleaded with them both. "It'll just make it worse." I paused long enough to catch my breath. "Keegan just gets out of hand sometimes. So, please, don't call them. My father, he'll . . ."

"Okay. We won't call them, all right?" Salvador's grandfather draped a lap blanket around my shoulders.

"Thank you," I squeaked out. But I wasn't sure if it was a thank you for the blanket, the kindness they now showed me, or for not call the police. Maybe it was for all three.

Grasping the edges, I cocooned my upper body inside the soft, fluffy warmth of the fabric. But it did little to rid me of the cold setting into my bones because I knew my father was gonna find out.

Maybe he already knows. The thought sent a shiver up my spine, making me shake.

"You're bleeding." Salvador eased my hand free of the blanket. "Where's it coming from?"

Fresh blood splotches marred the lap blanket where I had just held it.

Silently, Salvador inspected my fingers, hand, wrist, forearm, and then his gaze zoomed in on my fingers once again.

"You got some swelling on your pinky and ring

finger." He cupped my hand, his touch light and tender. "Can you move them?"

Other than the stiffness from the swelling and some moderate discomfort when moving my fingers, they seemed okay. So, I doubted anything had broken. But the dangling nail on my index finger smarted, and from what I could tell, was the source of the blood he had set out to investigate.

"Are you injured anywhere else?" His gaze roamed over my body.

Unable to trust my voice, I simply shook my head in response.

Truth be told, I'd had far worse than this at Keegan's hands. The man-child had a temper and never hesitated to use it.

"I'll put on some water for coffee, tea, coco, somethin' warm." His grandfather made his way to the kitchen, leaving me alone in the living room with Salvador.

A chime sounded, and Salvador fished his phone from his pocket. He two-thumbed another message, and before he could hit send, his cell rung.

"Javier. Where you at?" Salvador held the phone in front of him.

"Home. Why?" Javier's voice boomed through the speaker.

"Call the Russian *gringo*. Tell him that Keegan and

his crew paid me a little visit tonight."

"You guys, okay?" asked Javier. "You and Malibu?"

"Yeah, we're good. Banged up, but we're all right."

"What happened?"

"They tried to take her, but Grandpa threatened to blow their balls off. But if guessing, they'll be back. So, tell the Russian and Mina that I want eyes on her tomorrow while I'm gone."

"We can send her to the warehouse with the other girls or drop her off at the barn."

"Naw, man," said Salvador. "She's not going to either one of those."

"What? Why not?"

"Why? Because she's under my protection."

"Whatcha got in mind?"

"Let's just say, when we get back tomorrow, I'm gonna make sure he never touches her again."

"Fuckin' A!" Javier's voice rose in volume. "I can get onboard with that shit, and so will Clem, brother."

"No, you can't hurt him." My eyes watered, and tears spilled over my lower lids. "You don't understand. My father, he knows people. You can't—"

"Oh, but we can—I can." He caressed the side of my face, and instead of withdrawing, I leaned into his hand. "He should've never touched you, *mi pequeña paloma*."

18

Salvador

"I'm turnin' in, kids." Grandpa shuffled down the hallway to his room, shotgun in hand. "If ya need me, ya know where to find me. Come on, Zeus, you can bunk with me. Night."

"Goodnight, Mr. Vargas." Cindy pulled her legs under the blanket.

Zeus followed Grandpa like a second shadow, but *Estrello* remained in the living room on the couch, glued to Cindy's side.

"Did you mean what you said earlier?" She spoke her words in a soft whisper.

"I always say what I mean, *mi pequeña paloma.*" Channel surfing didn't reveal anything of interest, so

I left it on a cooking show. "But if there's something specific you want to discuss, I'm all ears."

Estrello opened his eyes and groaned, as if the discussion was keeping him from his beauty sleep. The cockblocker stretched out in the middle of the couch, laying his head against Cindy. And with his hind legs, he tried to shove me off the cushion I sat on.

"Look, about Keegan." And just like a flip of a switch, the plastic façade she wore at work, sheathed her facial features. "He's not really that bad. Keegan just has misguided anger."

"Misguided anger? Is that what it is? Misguided?"

"Yes. He doesn't mean the things he says or does. It's just the way he was brought up."

"Is that so?"

Her making light of Keegan's behavior only deepened my anger. No, my rage for the man.

"You'll see." A smile touched her lips, but it didn't reach her eyes. "Once he calms down, things will be better. He'll . . . he'll move on."

I wasn't sure if she was trying to sell that line of horseshit to me or herself. Or, just maybe, her family had conditioned her to think that way. Either way, bullshit was bullshit, and to me, it still smelled like a steaming pile of shit.

"Naw, see, that's where you're wrong," I said. "He

won't change unless he wants to. And what he did to you before . . . what he did at your apartment and here tonight, isn't unacceptable. Should never be acceptable. He's not a man, he's an angry boy pretending to be a man."

Gently, I tucked a loose lock of hair behind her ear.

"A real man knows how to treat a woman—how to cherish her." I freed her arm from the blanket just enough to expose the new bruises turning purple on her forearm. "And he sure as hell doesn't do this."

The blanket puckered open enough for me to get a glimpse of her lacy white bra, or what used to be white before her toss in the grass. My eyes roamed over her exposed pale skin, taking in her pink undertones. Figuring my gaze had lingered enough, I glanced up.

Dark circles made her eyelids appear dark. Crying had made the whites of her eyes red, which only made the blue of her irises pop more.

My phone buzzed in my front pocket. Even without looking, I knew who it was because it had to be one of three: Dominic, Javier, or Mina.

"I'm going to grab you something dry to put on, okay?"

Cindy pulled the blanket tight around her torso, then leaned her head against the back of the couch.

She drew in a deep breath, closed her eyes, then exhaled, slowly.

Estrello whined and snuggled closer to her. And I swear, a shit-eating-grin spread across the furry cockblocker's muzzle.

"Yeah, I see you, *Estrello*," I said to the hairy bastard licking his balls. "Don't get too comfortable cuz I'm coming back."

My words brought a smile to my little dove's lips that chased away some of the sadness in her eyes.

"Hey, stay here, and don't open the door for anyone. Okay?" I asked, then waited for a response.

She nodded.

"No one. Not even Javier, Clemente, or even Mina or her Russian. Understand?"

"Yes." She nodded once more. "Understood."

I took one last glance at *mi pequeña paloma*, then made my way down the hall to my bedroom. Once inside, I left the door open so I could hear if she called out.

My torn and dirty shirt stuck to my body, and the rain had soaked through every stitch of clothing I had on, making my pants stick to my nuts. Stripping out of my clothing, I toweled off, examined the bitch of a bruise over my bicep and ribs, then dressed.

For the size and color of the bruise, it didn't hurt

much, but it'd be stiff as fuck in the morning. Of that, I was certain.

I grabbed my phone and checked my messages.

A new one from Mina flashed across the screen.

—Stay with the girl tomorrow.

—You can run interference with the police.

—Whatever you need is at your disposal.

—Use your discretion.

I chewed on her words, digesting each one, then typed out a response.

—Thanks. I'll do that.

—What about tomorrow's project?

And by project, I meant the trade with her fucked-up uncle.

Three wavy lines let me know to expect a response any second.

—Stay. With. The. Girl.

—You can help her open the bar.

—I'll send some extra men.

With the swipe of my fingers, I scrolled through my list of contacts, then stopped at a single name, Filipe Sandoval.

The phone rang once, twice, three times, then the line clicked over.

"Hey. How is she?" asked Filipe with a musical tone in his voice.

"Shook up," I said. "I'm callin' in a favor."

"Oh, I think I know what kind." Filipe's words conveyed a smile. "Say no more. He won't bother her again. I guarantee it, brother."

19

Cindy

Buzz.

Buzz.

Buzz.

Fear crept in, coating my skin with the sensation of thousands of tiny spider legs crawling over my flesh. Goose bumps erupted, and I exhaled a ragged breath.

Either I answered the phone now or later, but either way, it was something I'd need to do.

Why put off tomorrow what you can do today?

I didn't even bother to read the name on the screen. It's not as if it would make a difference.

Keegan, my mother, my father, or his parents. It'd all be the same: wash, rinse, and repeat.

"Hello." I kept my voice at a steady-calm.

"Cindy, what have you done now?" The hysterics in my mother's voice never ceased to amaze me.

"Me? What do you mean? I've done nothing, Mother. What are you talking about?" Even before the question left my mouth, I knew exactly what she now referred to—the scrimmage that took place in the Vargas' front yard.

"Keegan's distraught, worried sick about you," she said.

"That's highly unlikely. He's just worried about his reputation—he's a lot like Dad in that way."

"He said you're held up with some gang member —that he has you on drugs. Maybe even into prostitution."

"Ha ha." The laughter slipped out before I could stop it. "Me, on drugs. Really? That's the pot calling the kettle black, don't you think?"

"Are you selling your body now?" Theatrical sobs thickened her voice. "Does he have you that hooked?"

I shouldn't bait her, draw her addiction out into the open, but at the moment, I just couldn't muster the strength, the energy, or the filter to tiptoe around the issue.

"Take a valium, Mother, then wash it down with a thumb or two of bourbon," I said. "Then you should feel better."

I should feel bad for the things I'm saying, thinking, because she's as much a victim of my father—if not more so—than I am.

Neither she nor I wanted this life, didn't choose it. Nope. Powerful, influential men choose it for us.

Men who kept mayors, senators, and top-notch politicians in their back pockets and at their beck and call.

"You need to come," she said, turning up the waterworks a notch or two. "Get back on the right track. Then you'll see things differently."

"Differently. What, you mean like you? Like Dad, Grandpa, and the other men at the firm?" I asked. "Nope. Not gonna happen. I'm not interested in the Kool-Aid being served."

The clap of a slap sounded, followed by a feminine shriek.

It was a familiar sound. One I'd grown up with over the years. So, I braced myself for what would come next—what always came next—the blind rage.

"You listen up, and you listen well," shouted my father. "You will come home. You will patch things up with Keegan. And you will marry him. Do you hear me?"

I let the residual echo of his voice on the cell die out.

"Did you hear me?"

"Yeah. I heard you, Dad."

"Well?"

"No." The single word felt good leaving the tip of my tongue.

"No?" His voice dropped several octaves. "What do you mean, no?"

"I mean just what I said. No." I repeated the word, knowing it would set him off. "No, to going home. No, to making up with Keegan. And most defiantly no, to marrying him. No. As in, it's not happening, none of it."

"You come home, and do as I say, or I will cut you off. Do you hear me?" he shouted. "All financial support, gone. Is that what you want?"

"If it means cutting you out of my life like a cancerous mass, then yes, that's what I want."

"Don't test my limits. I will cut you off."

"Do it." My body shook. I wasn't sure if it was from the cold, anger, fear, or from the empowerment of standing up to my father. "You cut me from your life long ago. Even turned me into a pawn for you to wield as you saw fit. But it's over."

"It's not over until I say it's over. Your mother and I brought you into this world, you ungrateful little bitch, and I can wipe you off it any time I want. Do you hear me?"

"Fine. Then consider me dead and buried." My index finger tapped the red "x" on the phone, hanging up the call.

I guess this is fair all the way around, I thought. *He's been dead to me for years.*

20

Salvador

"That sounded rough." I motioned to her phone.

"How much did you hear?"

"More than perhaps I should have. Sorry."

"No. It's okay." She drew in a deep breath, then let it out slowly. "It's been a long time in coming."

"Here." I handed her the dry clothing. "It's all I got."

"Thanks." A small smile played on her lips. "I appreciate it."

The moment she rose, a groan left her lips, and pain flittered across her eyes. She drew her arm to her chest, cradling it.

"Go change." I motioned to the door. "And I'll see

what I can find to take the edge off that injured hand of yours."

"Okay." She made her way to the bathroom with a slight limp. "Hey, Sal."

"Yeah."

"Thanks."

"Don't mention it. Happy to help."

"Now, go, get out of those wet clothes."

She shot one more glance in my direction, then entered the bathroom, closing the door behind her.

Making my way down the hallway in the dark, I entered my grandfather's room. Zeus' head popped up from the foot of the bed. He yawned, then buried his head in the covers.

The rhythmic sound of my grandfather's CPAC machine drummed on and on.

My gaze darted to the nightstand next to his bed. Using my phone as a flashlight, I glanced at the bottles stacked in neat rows. The fourth bottle in, I found what I had come for, Tylenol 3, prescribed for glaucoma.

The bottle, filled more than four months ago, remained almost full. He didn't like taking medication that dulled his senses. Said he didn't want to sleep or let life pass him by in a stupor, so he chose the pain over medication.

Pain lets you know you're in the land of the living,

Son, he once said to me right after the death of my parents. *So don't fear it. Embrace it.*

I opened the bottle, extracted a couple of pills, then resealed it. With care, I placed the bottle back in its original resting spot. Not because he'd be angry that I took them. He'd gladly give the shirt off his back to help another living soul. It was just that he was a stickler when it came to things having their place and everything remaining in its place.

A quick glance around his orderly room brought a smile to my lips. The man had OCD issues, but at least he used the compulsive behavior in positive ways. Just for general purposes, and maybe even as a display of my own OCD tendencies, I checked the locks on his windows, ensuring the security of the room.

Out in the hallway, I entered my room, checking those windows as well, then moved into the kitchen and living room, doing the same.

One can't be too careful. My father had once said to me.

And he was right. I had more than myself to consider. I now had my grandfather and Cindy to protect.

Back in the living room, I spotted her curled in one of the corners of the couch. The little cock-blocker, *Estrello,* remained at her side.

"Move." My command went unanswered. *"Estrello*, get off the sofa."

Still nothing. The dog was stubborn as fuck.

Just like his owner, Isa, the thought made me grin. *Yeah, Augustin had his hands full with that one.*

"Outside?" The moment the single word left my lips, *Estrello* made a mad dash for the back door.

By the time I got there, Zeus had joined him.

"Not sure how you heard me, boy," I said to Zeus. "That CPAC is loud as fuck," I whispered, then opened the door. "Go on. Do your thing."

I shut the door, leaving them out for a bit. In the kitchen, I grabbed a bottle of water, then returned to the living room.

"Here." I handed her the pills. "Take these."

"What are they?"

"Pain meds." I twisted the top off the water bottle. "You can wash them down with this."

She hesitated for a moment. "It's not Vicodin, right?"

"Naw. Why?"

"I'm allergic."

"Tylenol 3. It'll take the edge off."

"Thanks." She tossed the pills in her mouth, grabbed the water, then took three large gulps.

"Tired?"

"A little," she said. "But I don't think I can sleep yet."

Sitting next to her, I turned on the television. A cooking show sprung to life.

I pressed my back into the couch. A few minutes into the show, Cindy leaned her head against my shoulder. Putting an arm around her, I drew her body next to mine.

Not gonna lie. I liked the way her curves molded against me.

"Sleep," I whispered, then kissed the top of her head. "I got you. You're safe with me."

And I meant it. She was safe. I wouldn't let anything, or anyone—including her family or Keegan—come between me and *mi pequeña paloma*.

21

Cindy

An electric whirling noise sounded in the distance, and a steady cadence thumped in my ear.

A boom, followed by barking, made my eyelids flutter, then spring open. Startled, my body flinched, and a soft yelp left my lips.

"It's only the dogs," a familiar voice whispered.

The warmth of Salvador's body pressed against my side and cheek felt comforting. Tipping my head, I locked eyes with him. It was then I placed the thumping—his heartbeat.

"Sorry." I was slow to move. "Must've fallen asleep."

"I didn't mind." A smile split his lips.

When I sat upright, he rose.

"I'll be back." He headed toward the kitchen. "Gonna, let the dogs inside."

"What time is it?" I glanced at the television.

A chef in a gourmet kitchen chopped a large yellow onion, set it aside, then diced some green bell pepper.

The tippity-tap of dog nails met my ears, and seconds later, two wet, cold noses pressed against me. Zeus sniffed my toes, and *Estrello* inspected my injured hand, then tried to lick my fingers.

"I'm okay, buddy." I patted his head, then Zeus'. "Just a sprain. Nothing that a bit of rest can't solve."

A yawn hit, and I stifled the noise with the back of my other hand.

"Tired?" asked Salvador.

"Yeah." I rose from the couch.

My surroundings backed out, and my body felt weightless.

"Whoa." Strong arms wrapped around my body. "You okay?"

"Uhm, I think so." My body felt like puddy. "Just a bit swimming. Got up too fast, I think."

"You're a lightweight, aren't you?" asked Salvador.

"What?" His words didn't make any sense.

"The medication," he said. "It hit you hard."

"Oh, that, yeah." I laid my head on his shoulder, relishing the warmth and comfort it provided. "I have a low tolerance. Which is why I don't drink."

"How about I help you?" He scooped me up in his arms.

"Okay." A giggle passed my lips

My arms looped around his neck, and I breathed in the way he smelled.

"I like your cologne. It's nice."

"Good to know." He chuckled.

The thump of his beating heart lulled me. It offered comfort and safety. Two things I hadn't felt in a long time.

Inside his bedroom, he pulled back the covers, then sat me on the bed.

"In you go." Salvador lifted the sheet, waiting for me to slide under it. "Call if you need anything." He tucked me in, then turned to leave.

"Lay with me." The fingers of my good hand wrapped around his arm, stopping his forward momentum.

He held my gaze for several seconds, his face an unreadable mask.

"Please. I don't want to be alone."

"Scoot over." He motioned for me to move, so I scooted to the other side of his full-sized bed.

The mattress shifted with the weight of his body, and I found myself migrating toward the comfort of his warmth. He wrapped his arm around me and drew my back to his chest. Cradled in his arms, it didn't bother me that we now spooned.

Salvador made me feel safe, protected.

"Sal."

"Yeah." His warm breath blew over my neck.

"Why don't you have a girlfriend?" My body stiffened. "I'm sorry, that was an internal question. I didn't mean to ask that. I uhm . . ."

"It's okay." He chuckled. "Hadn't met the right girl yet."

Hadn't. He had used the word hadn't. *Does that mean he's interested in someone?*

"So, you *'hadn't met the right girl yet,'* so does that mean that now you've met her?"

"Could be." He nestled his face against the back of my neck. "How'd you met Keegan?"

"Uhm, dear 'ol Dad arranged that."

"What do you mean?"

"My family and Keegan's go way back. And I do mean way, way back." I exhaled a heavy sigh. "Our grandfathers knew each other. Even started the firm together."

"What does that have to do with you dating Keegan—or being engaged to him?"

"I'm. Not. Engaged!" Irritation coated my words. "Never was."

"Okay. Sorry. Didn't mean to pick at a sore spot."

"No. I'm the one who should be sorry. I shouldn't have snapped at you." I snuggled closer to the warmth of his body. "We went to private school together, and then to the same college. Over the years, his parents and mine kept tossing Keegan and I together: summer trips, combined family vacations, he was everywhere. So, dating in college seemed like the next step. But only it wasn't."

"What do you mean?"

"Keegan was okay as a friend. But the moment we started dating, he wanted more."

"More what?"

"More of everything. To have me. To own me. To control me. To be top of his class—so I did his work. Actually, did everything he and my parents wanted me to? But it wasn't enough. He wanted more: to land a prestigious spot in a law firm, which he was born into because he has a penis and balls. And, well, let's just say, he only knows how to take and take and take . . ."

My body shook.

"I'm sorry." Salvador tightened his hold. "I didn't mean to upset you."

"It's not your fault." Rolling around, I faced him. "You didn't do anything wrong. He did."

Tears brimmed my eyes.

22

Salvador

"If you need space to figure out what you want, Cindy, I can give that to you."

"What if I don't want space?" She swallowed hard. "What if I know what I want?"

I tucked a lock of hair behind her ear.

"What if I want you?" Her eyes held a vulnerability, an innocence that drew me in like a moth to a flame.

"Is that what you want?"

She nodded.

"Then tell me what you want—what you need."

"I want . . . I want you to hold me. To kiss me. To touch me."

Her words were music to my ears.

Drawing her into my arms, I claimed her lips. She tasted sweet, like my personal slice of heaven, and I wasn't sure how I'd ever get enough of her.

She laced her fingers in my hair, toying with the loose waves.

When I broke the kiss, it left her breathless. Her quick breaths pressed her torso against me, and even through the clothing, I felt the pebbling of her nipples.

I slid a hand under the shirt and caressed her back, surprised to find she had left her bra off.

Her eyes, so clear and trusting, pulled me in. Rolling her on to her back, I covered her body with mine. The way she fit under me, curves molding to mine, felt perfect, as if she were made for me.

She ground her hips against me, and the words she'd spoken earlier replayed in my mind: *I want you to hold me. To kiss me. To touch me.*

Mi pequeña paloma needed me, and I wasn't about to let her down. Not now, not ever.

Drawing in a deep breath, I breathed in her unique smell: melon and peach scent with a hint of mint.

I could smell her all day and die a happy man. But right now, I needed more.

A need to touch her, taste her, make her come,

had me leaving a trail of hot kisses down her neck. Pushing up the shirt, I unearthed a white, creamy breast with an erect little bud, and my mouth watered.

The moment my mouth covered her breast, a moan rolled off her lips. Just the thought that she wanted me, desired me, made me want to please her. So I slid down her body, leaving more kisses in my wake. The way her muscles rippled under my mouth, under my tongue, made me wonder just how receptive my little dove would be to my touch.

Taking hold of the waistband of the oversized sweats, I eased them down her leg and tossed them to the floor, only to find a clean-shaven mound.

I rubbed my nose against her, breathing her in, and a groan passed my lips.

Fuck, I thought. *If I don't regain control, I'll shoot my wad like some sex-starved teen.*

Slowly, I eased her legs apart, then made my way up, nipping, licking, and tasting her. Inches from her mound, I breathed her.

I'd never smelled anything as appetizing or mouthwatering as the woman splayed before me.

A thought came to me. *If she tastes as good as she smells, I'm in trouble.*

With my thumbs, I split her open, then pressed my tongue against her inner moist folds. Her hips bucked forward, and she tried to press her legs together, which only brought her thighs against my shoulders.

"Sal." Her voice cracked. "What are you . . ."

"Relax," I whispered. "I just want to taste you."

The tip of my tongue flicked the erect little acorn hiding under the hood of her clit.

"Oh, God." Her hips shot forward again, almost toppling me from my perch.

"*Mi pequeña paloma.*" I held her gaze with a grin. "Try not to move."

"I'm trying. I promise, I am."

"Has anyone ever touched you like this? Brought you to an orgasm through oral?"

Her eyes widened, and she shook her head.

I shouldn't be surprised, but I was. With a body as receptive as hers—one made for worshiping— only a fool wouldn't feast on all she had to offer.

A fuckin' fool named Keegan Fuckin' Black.

"Then lay back, so I can enjoy your body with you."

She pressed her head against the pillow but kept her wide-eyed stare trained on me. I looped my arms around her thighs, pinning her to the bed. Spreading her wet folds with my thumbs once more, I licked her, starting first with the tight little hole of her anus, then across the opening my cock

161

desired entry into, then finished the journey to her clit.

Her taste coated my tongue, making my mouth water. And only one thought filled my mind.

She had to come undone against my mouth, my tongue. So, I got to work licking, flicking, and sucking to find what her body responded to most.

Rolling my tongue over her swollen clit made her thighs tremble, so I applied more pressure.

Little mews of pleasure escaped her lips, urging me on.

I pressed my mouth to her, creating a seal, then sucked. Releasing her right leg, I slid a finger across her wet folds, then plunged it inside her.

Her hips bucked, her body trembled, and her muscles contracted around my finger.

Mi pequeña paloma came against my lips, and I continued to stroke her with my tongue, lapping up every drop of her arousal.

When her body stilled, I slid up next to her, then drew her into my arms.

"You okay." The taste of her lingered on my lips.

"Uh-huh." She pressed her body against mine, then kissed my lips. "What about you?"

She ground her hips, rubbing my hard as fuck cock.

"Me, I'm good." I took in the afterglow on her

face, caused by the orgasm. "Tomorrow's gonna be a long day."

As much as I wanted to fuck her, I needed to take my time and focus on her and her needs. But already, the desire to taste her, to feel her coming apart against my tongue left me wanting more.

I want her—all of her—heart, body, and soul.

23

Cindy

Four beige walls surround me, closing in.

Thoughts of last night—the front yard, namely—came to mind. I squeezed my eyes shut, trying to push away the negative thoughts.

It finally happened. *My father has disowned me.*

A nervous energy hummed on the surface of my skin, making me feel as if my whole body buzzed.

It's what I always wanted, right?

A part of me mourned the loss of family. But the other side, the logical one, crooned on my shoulder.

Good riddance. All's well that ends well.

It was going to happen at some point, sooner or

later, but somehow, I always thought it'd occur later, much later. But has it really ended?

Am I free? Or is freedom only an illusion, an unattainable mirage?

The thought of being tied to Keegan by marriage and with kids used to terrify me—scared the living hell out of me. So, waking in Salvador's arm and actually wanting something 'more' with him, really confused me this morning.

How can I want freedom from one man, yet let another claim me in a budding relationship?

Unable to go back to sleep or shut down my racing mind, I opted for the next best thing—getting up. But between Salvador spooning me, *Estrello* stealing more than half my pillow, and Zeus warming my feet, I didn't have a clue what to do.

Inching my way up the bed like an inchworm, I managed to pull myself to a sitting position. Zeus didn't open an eye, move, or even groan when my legs slid out from under him. *Estrello*, on the other hand, opened an eye and arched a doggy brow.

Arm extended, I signed the word for move like I'd seen Isa do hundreds of times, and to my surprise, he obeyed.

Once free of the bed, I did a quick sweep of the room, looking for the sweats Salvador had given me to wear. Once located, I step into them, then secured the drawstring to keep them in place. Thoughts of what had occurred last night came to mind, and a grin touched my lips. The way Salvador had touched me made my body feel, well, it was just short of a miracle in my book.

Never in a million years would I have ever guessed Salvador and I would share an intimate moment.

He makes me feel alive, seen. Salvador evokes an unbridled passion deep within me.

A deep-seated throb hit my clit at the thought of the way his tongue, his mouth, felt on my body. I'd never experienced anything remotely like it. And now, it's the only thing I can really think about.

I'd always looked at Salvador from afar. But like an elusive score of music to decipher, or a priceless art relic, he always seemed unreachable—unattainable. In all the months I'd seen him at the bar, I had never once seen him with a female. Plus, he hadn't hooked up with any of the barmaids or employees.

For a while, I wondered if he even liked women. But after coming to my aid yesterday, and the skilled way he worked my body and brought me to a mind-blowing orgasm, clearly, he liked females.

A glance at my phone had my eyes rolling. I had fifty-seven missed calls, more than thirty of them from Keegan. The electronic device vibrated, and a text came through—the sender, my mother.

—Are you happy now?

—He froze your accounts and mine.

—You're not only hurting yourself.

—You're hurting me.

—Please reconsider.

—Come home!

There were so many things I wanted to say to her, to all of them, but what good would it do? She had made her bed and had stayed in the middle of it.

Her lifestyle isn't mine.

Without hesitation, I shutdown my phone, then removed the sim card.

The information on there about my father's partner, Keegan's father, and the mayor came to mind. It's amazing what one learns when hiding in the shadows.

You've always like 'em young, haven't ya, Keegan's father had joked with the mayor, and my father's response had left a dark mark on my soul: *the next time you want some pussy, make sure it's legal and consensual. Better yet, let us know, and we'll provide it.*

I drew in a shaky breath.

Bile slid into the back of my throat, and I swallowed hard, forcing it back down. My father wasn't an affectionate man, never had been, but I'd never pegged him for aiding and abetting a rapist.

An insurance policy. I held the sim card between my fingers, then slipped it into the pocket of the sweats I wore. Later, I'd find a hiding place for it, but until then, I'd keep it close.

My gaze flicked to the trashcan, and I tossed my cell inside. Once at the bar, and when on a break, I'd walk next door to the mobile center and grab a cheap phone with a month-to-month plan.

My stomach grumbled.

Pushing thoughts of my father, Keegan, and the others out of my mind, I glanced around the kitchen. As expected, pots, pans, and skillets occupied the oven along with a grill. A well-stocked refrigerator brought a smile to my face.

Eggs, milk, bacon, butter, juice, and an array of jams came into view.

A quick peek in the pantry revealed flour, vanilla, baking powder, and iodized salt.

Mmm. Pancakes. My mouth watered. Grabbing a bowl and the ingredients needed, I got to work.

24

Salvador

Wet, slurping sounds roused me from a dead sleep.

My eyelids sprung open. Seconds later, I locked gazes with the source. The little cockblocker who felt right at home licking his dick on my bed.

"What the . . ." I grabbed a pillow, then chunked it at him. "Get off. Go do that somewhere else."

The impact didn't even faze him. Without missing a stroke, his tongue wrapped around his ball sack, then slid back into his mouth.

A quick glance of my room alerted me to the fact something was missing, or more importantly, a someone, *mi pequeña paloma.*

Rising, I stretched my arms overhead, working

the kinks out of my neck and back. A groan left my lips at the slight tinge of pain and stiffness in my arm and the heavy ache centered on the bruised area of my ribs.

Yep, payback's gonna be a bitch.

Reaching for my cell on the nightstand caused me to groan once more. Several unread messages waited for me.

I read them in the order that they had hit, starting with Filipe's.

—Your package arrived this morning.

—What should I do with it?

It took all fuckin' night, but he and his crew had found the slimy, flaky fucker. A bit of adrenaline rushed through my body, waking me faster than a concentrated, double hit of espresso.

—Hold on to it.

—Keep it contained.

—Stored in a dry, cool place.

—I'll meet you at RH tonight.

And by cool, I meant to chain that fucker up at the River House inside the barn. When I got done with that little prick, Keegan Black, he'd either be reborn or gator bait.

Dominic's message and Mina's seemed to mirror one another. Both wanting to make sure I kept my eyes on *mi pequeña paloma,* as if anyone could drag me away now, and handle the bar without making waves.

Ring.

Ring.

Ring.

Spider's name flickered across the screen.

"Yeah," I said, answering the phone.

"The boss lady wants to make sure you know the plan and your role in it," Spider's calm and collective Italian accent crooned over the line. "So, ya know the plan?"

"I read the texts."

"Good. Then you know it's the plan where you stay with Miss Stevens at the bar," said Spider. "You'll make sure all runs well there today, yes?"

"Yeah. Got it."

"Are you sure you got it?"

"Yeah, that's what I said. Why?"

Spider drew in a deep breath, then exhaled loudly. "Because a little birdie mentioned to Marco that you have a package to attend to. One *Chiquita,* the boss lady, knows nothing about."

"My package isn't of concern—not yours or hers to worry about." A spark of anger grew.

"Ahh, but you're wrong," said Spider. "All affairs are of her concern. You know this."

"Not this one."

"Oh, but again, you are wrong. This package is of top priority. And as such, *Chiquita,* will advise what to do with it when she returns," said Spider. "She expects it to remain in mint condition. Understood?"

Fuck! I clenched a fist. "Fine. But what occurs after . . . well, let's just say shit happens."

I shot off a text to Filipe.

—Keep the package in one piece

—Unblemished. Mint condition.

Fuck me. I didn't like others in my business. *It makes shit messy.*

Three wavy lines hit the screen, letting me know a reply was on its way.

—One piece isn't an issue.

—But it had some wear and tear.

Shit, one thing at a time. I needed to remain focused.

The moment I step into the hallway, the cock-blocker—now finished cleaning his balls—pranced to the kitchen.

"Sneaky little bastard," I whispered.

It's not that I didn't like animals, actually, I've always liked dogs. Even had one as a little *chamaco*. But the fact that *Estrello* felt a need to come between me and *mi pequeña paloma* was becoming an issue.

One I needed to nip in the butt much sooner than later.

Halfway across the hallway, the whiff of bacon and fresh coffee tickled my nose.

"Come on then, I'll let you out," my grandfather's voice carried down the walkway.

The sound of the back door opening, then closing, hit my ears along with a light, feminine hum. Her words remained just out of reach.

Rounding the corner, I kept my steps as silent as possible, not wanting to alert Cindy to my presence. A quick search and I discovered my grandfather outside with the dogs.

Across the room, Cindy commanded the kitchen, flipping pancakes, checking on the sizzling bacon, and cooking scrambled eggs.

I made my way to the table unnoticed, then took a seat to enjoy the show.

A few minutes went by then, upon my grandfather's reentry, the dogs bounced across the room.

Zeus stopped in front of me while Estrello approached Cindy, who flipped over another pancake.

She turned and locked eyes with me. A smile spread across her face, brightening her eyes.

"Well, lookie there," said Grandpa. "Another world heard from."

"Morning, Grandpa."

"Why didn't you wake me when you got up?" I rose and headed for the cabinet to retrieve a mug.

"I figured you needed the sleep." She plated a stack of pancakes, then added bacon and scrabbled eggs. "Ya hungry?"

"Yeah." My eyes roamed over her body. "I am."

I'm hungry for more than food, mi pequeña paloma.

25

Cindy

"Did yawl want more eggs?" The gusto in which Salvador and his grandfather ate surprised me.

"No, thank you." Mr. Vargas waved off the offer. A playful grin played on his lips. "I'm watching the figure."

"I'm good." Salvador eyed the plate of cooked pancakes. "But I'll take a couple more of those." He plopped a piece of bacon into his mouth.

His grandfather leaned back, coffee in hand. "So, what will you kids do today?"

"Me," I said, gathering my plate, fork, and mug. "I've got an early morning shift at The Alchemist."

Flipping the water on, I rinsed the items in the sink. "Been putting off inventory for a while."

"And today's the lucky day?" asked Mr. Vargas, then he turned to Salvador. "And what about you? What's your boss lady got ya doin'?"

"Got some stuff to take care of at the bar." Salvador took a healthy bite of what remained of his second stack of pancakes.

"Oh, hey." I glanced over a shoulder. "Do you mind taking me by my place? I, uhm, I need to check on things and change. Or I can request an Uber if you're—"

"No, to an Uber. So don't even think about it," said Salvador. "Yes, to taking you by your place." He washed the last of his food down with a few swigs of coffee. "Gotta check on the work done there yesterday."

"Work?" I had a hard time computing the meaning of his words. "What work?"

"I had a crew go out to your place," Salvador replied. "They cleaned and secured it. Replaced the door, reinforced the windows, and . . ." He checked the screen of his phone. "They're setting up the security system this morning—as we speak."

"Security? A system?" *When had I agreed to the installation of a security system?* "I never said . . . I never agreed to—"

"Mina approved it." Salvador rose, slipped his cell in his front pocket, acting as if the current conversation was a natural discussion.

"Oh, so . . ." I kept my tone neutral. "So, because she approved it, that makes it okay?" One of my brows arched in question.

Mr. Vargas chuckled silently and seemed to try hiding the fact he now laughed.

"Mina, like everyone else—including me—wants to make sure you're safe. And if that means implementing some extra safety conditions, then so be it. I don't see an issue."

"You don't see an issue?" The dishes clanged inside the sink.

"Oh, you need to think before you speak, Son." He nudged Salvador with an elbow. "It's been a while, but I recognize that tone of warning."

Salvador's gaze flicked from mine to his grandfather, then to mine once more.

His creamy, milk chocolate-colored eyes roamed over my frame as if seeing me for the first time. I was used to men looking at me, but what I wasn't used to was the sensation of actually being seen. And after what he'd done last night . . . what I'd allowed him to do to my body. I wasn't entirely sure what to think.

What if he thinks I do stuff like that all the time? The

thought mortified me. "Look, you can't just bark orders at people or make decisions without me."

"Bark orders?" Salvador leaned against the counter. "Is that what you think I'm doing? Barking?"

"Yes. I mean no." I rinsed his plate and his grandfather's. "Look, I'm talking about having people work at my place without asking me first. That kind of stuff."

"Well, yesterday, you gave me the go-ahead to have the guys secure your place, which included removing debris and any potential threats," said Salvador. "Adding security measures takes care of the latter, don't you think?"

He had a point. I had given him the all-clear to 'secure' the area, as he put it, but I guess his idea of what that meant and mine differed.

Is that such a bad thing? I chewed on the thought. I figured he'd have one of the guys board the entrance until a suitable replacement for the door was made.

The tip of his pink tongue slid over his full lips, drawing my attention to his mouth.

An awkward silence filled the surrounding air.

"Well, kids, I'm gonna leave ya to the rest of your day." Mr. Vargas headed toward the hallway, stopped, then said over his shoulder, "Will you two be here for dinner tonight?"

"Naw." Salvador shook his head, never breaking eye contact with me. "She has a thing—we have a thing tonight."

"Just as well." His gaze flicked from me to Salvador. "I won't be home either. I'm gonna help your *Tia* rehang a door this evening."

"Don't tell me it's the bathroom again," Salvador said with a sigh.

"Yep." Nodded Mr. Vargas. "Torn clean off the hinges again."

"*¡Híjole!*" Salvador shook his head. "If you have a hard time, wait, and I'll help you tomorrow, okay?"

"Yeah. All right. But I think *Tia* and I can manage." Mr. Vargas disappeared down the hall to his bedroom.

Silence fell over the kitchen once more.

"Hey, *Mejo*," Mr. Vargas called. "I need to borrow your Jeep."

"What's wrong with your truck?"

"The starter's out," replied Mr. Vargas. "Andres said he'd replace it this coming weekend."

"Andres or Alejandro?" asked Salvador.

"One of them," his grandfather said. "Can never tell them apart. One looks like the other." He gave a dismissive wave of his hand.

"I can drop you off at *Tia's* house on the way to the bar."

"Need to drive," replied Mr. Vargas. "Your Tia needs some groceries and supplies for the wedding."

"I need to take Cindy by her place, then drive to the club."

"Hey, don't w-worry about me." I dried my hands. "I can Uber."

"No," said Salvador in a firm tone. "You can't."

"I'm a big girl. I can—"

"Have you forgotten about your run-in with Keegan so soon?" His words incited goose bumps to prickle my flesh, and my mouth went dry.

"What? No."

"I can have my grandfather drop us off, then see if Clemente or Javier or one of the Torres brothers are still in town to pick us up."

A thought came to mind. "What about your motorcycle?"

"What about it?"

"We could take that, you know, so your grandfather could take your Jeep." A small smile hit my lips. "I mean, if that'd be okay."

26

Salvador

The heat of her body pressed to mine had my dick thinking about all kinds of things. Namely, what it'd feel like sheathed inside her warmth. Originally, I wasn't thrilled about transporting her on my wheels, but hey, now, I had changed my mind.

Back at her place, the twenty minutes it took her to shower, dress, and get ready, I'd walked through her place, assessed the remaining damage, the work completed, inspected the new reinforced door, and approved the security measures put in place.

Hell, I even had time to log into the security network to monitor the interior and exterior. So, if a

Jehovah's Witnesses knocked on her door, I'd sure as shit know about it.

I rounded the corner of the parking lot, swung behind the building, then drove into the attached delivery hub of The Alchemist.

Once I shut off the engine, then stabilized my wheels, I offered *mi pequeña paloma* a hand.

"Remember how to get off?" I asked.

"Yes." She released her hold, and I missed the feel of her body pressed against mine.

Thoughts of last night crossed my mind. The way she had squirmed, panted, and come undone at my touch had me wanting to taste her once again.

Once she got off, I then removed my helmet—handing it to her—secured my wheels, then unlocked the back entrance to the club.

"You said you've got a lot of inventory to do?" I made my way down the hallway to Mina's office.

"Yeah," she followed me inside the office, then shut the door. "Mina's wanting to add some new additions to the menu."

"So, that requires a complete inventory?" I used my phone to turn on lights in different parts of the building, namely, in the stockrooms.

"Well, yeah." She nodded. "Wait, are we the only ones here?"

"Yep."

She leaned over the arm of the couch and set the helmets on one corner. The jeans she'd slipped on after her shower this morning hugged the curves of her hips and cupped her heart-shaped ass.

"Is that an issue?" I drew her into my arms.

To my surprise, she didn't pull away. Instead, she relaxed and leaned into me.

"Will you need help to catalog anything?" I asked. "Or some muscle for heavy lifting?"

"No." She shook her head. "I'm only doing a visual count. I want to see what beverages move faster than others."

"Do you need to pull numbers from one of the mainframes?"

"Nope." She wiggled her phone at eye level. "I can access the system from here and enter real-time data. That way, I can formulate a plan to see how often to stock each one. Automation is the goal."

"That's good and all, but how do you plan to automate the process?"

"By cataloging the content and adding barcodes. That way, bartenders and staff can scan a product out each time they take something."

"Nice." My girl had brains, and that made her sexy as fuck.

"And as long as inventory remains accurate, I can

set the parameters on how and when to order for restocking."

I drew her closer, my face inches from hers. The moment her arms looped around my neck, and she pressed her lips to mine, I claimed her mouth.

The phone in my pocket buzzed against the shaft of my semi-hard dick. Slipping it out, I checked the screen.

Damn. The Russian had fucked up timing.

"Yeah." The phone pressed to my ear. I waited for him to speak.

"You hear from JC or the Torres brothers?" He had a clipped tone to his speech.

"Naw, man." I had a feeling things were about to turn to shit and fast. "What's up?"

"A cluster fuck," replied the Russian. "That's what!"

"Give me a moment," I said into the phone, then turned to *mi pequeña paloma.* "Why don't you start on that inventory?" I winked at her. "When done here, I'll come find you."

"Oh, uhm, o-okay." The uncertainty in her voice made me feel like a shit because I was fairly certain she'd heard what the Russian had said.

The sway of her hips grabbed my attention, and I watched her sashay out of the office.

Once the patter of her shoes no longer hit my ears, I let out a heavy sigh.

Two words left my mouth, "Define clusterfuck!"

"Give me the phone," Mina's voice chimed in. "You heard from JC or the Torres brothers?"

"Naw. Why?" I didn't like the direction this call had taken.

"My cunt-of-an-uncle thought a round of fuckin' Red Rover would be fun."

"And?" I prompted her.

"During the exchange, the fucker asked for JC and Jorge to 'come on over,' like they were on the Price Is Fuckin' Right!" Her scoff sounded more like a growl. "During the exchange, we ambushed his men, but the fucker had men waiting."

"And?" I was nearing the end of my patience.

"Once the fucking damn broke . . ." her voice grew distant, and masculine groans of pain sounded.

I was at an impasse, a gridlock of information, and I needed some fuckin' answers, and soon.

"Hey," said the Russian. "Mina's indisposed at the moment."

"What the fuck is going on?" I barely contained my composure.

"JC, Jorge, and the Torres brothers haven't checked in," said the Russian. "Last time I saw them was through my scope. I took out several of the Mad

Dog's men, laying cover, but I couldn't tell where they all scattered."

"And by scattered, you mean what?"

"I mean just that," replied the Russian. "They scattered into the pasture at the neutral zone."

"Fuck me!"

"That's not all."

"Oh, there's more?"

"Yeah," said the Russian. "Get the doc. We're gonna need him." A couple of seconds ticked by. "We got two wounded."

"Son-of-a . . . Shit." I let out a breath.

A cluster fuck doesn't even begin to explain this shit!

27

Cindy

"Wait." A frigid frost chilled the marrow in my bones. "No one has seen Juan Carlos or the Torres brothers?"

"You shouldn't have been eavesdropping." His face wore an emotionless mask.

"Sal." I entered the office, holding an arm to my chest. "What's going on?"

"I could ask you the same question." His gaze focused on my hand, or more importantly to the blood-soaked paper towel wrapped around the tip of the ring finger of my left hand.

"This," I waved my hand at eye level. "This is nothing. A small nick."

He rose from behind Mina's desk, then approached me.

The mask void of emotion vanished, replaced by a warmth of concern in his milk chocolate eyes. Cupping my hand with one of his, he gently unwrapped my finger, examining the cut.

"How'd it happen?" he asked.

"Oh, uhm." Standing in front of him, the warmth of his body beckoned me closer. "Cut it on a plastic strap around a box. It caught my finger when I pulled the strap to snap it off."

"Come here." He coaxed me to the couch. "Now, sit."

He crossed the room, grabbed a little first aid kit, then returned to me.

"Doc's on his way, but I think I can handle this one." He winked.

Salvador flipped the case open, then grabbed some saline spray.

"What are you . . ."

"Gonna clean it, then dress it."

"Oh, look at you." A smile fluttered on my lips. "Mr. Boy Scout playing doctor."

"Actually, I was a boy scout." He got to work cleaning the cut.

"You were not."

"I was." He applied firm pressure, but not enough

to hurt me. "It's still bleeding a bit."

After a few minutes, he released his hold. He examined the superficial wound, wrapped a Band-Aid over it, then placed a light kiss over my thumb.

Salvador's gaze focused on my mouth, then flicked to my eyes. Bowing his head, he placed a chaste kiss to first my left cheek, then the right, before moving on to my lips.

His kiss, unrushed and tender, made my heart flutter in my chest. The way he skillfully moved his lips over mine brought to mind what he had done the night before.

A heat spread between my legs, and my clit throbbed with arousal. Two things that, until last night, had never happened. Sex with Keegan had been just an act, a physical motion of two bodies that I hadn't felt a connection to, nor was it something I had sought out. But now, with the way I felt—the way Salvador had made me feel—I wanted to feel him next to me, inside me.

Heat warmed my face, and I pulled away from the kiss to draw in a breath.

"What's on your mind?" His hooded brown eyes kept me pinned in place. "Anything good I should know about?"

"I uhm . . ." I held his dreamy, lust-filled gaze.

He cupped my chin, then caressed my lower lip with the pad of his thumb.

His phone chimed. Salvador checked the screen, pressed his forehead to mine, then let out a deep sigh.

"We've got company," he whispered. "And they're coming in hot."

"Hot?" His choice of words confused me. "What does that even mean?"

"Come with me." He grabbed my good hand, laced his fingers with mine, then headed for the doorway leading to the hall.

In the storage area, not far from where the delivery entrance sat, a collage of footsteps fell, echoing on top of one another.

"Lay him down flat," Mina's voice boomed over the drumming on the floor.

"Goddamn." Augustin's voice sounded strained. "Let go of my leg, you hulking, Neanderthal fuck."

"Over here," shouted Spider. "Someone hit the lights."

"Got 'em," Marciano crooned.

Lights flooded the stockroom floor.

Salvador's abrupt stop had me slamming against his back with a groan. He wrapped a hand around my waist to keep me steady.

"Towels. Get me some towels," shouted Dominic.

Mina glanced around. "Where's Rafa?"

"The doc's on his way," replied Salvador. "ETA in under five minutes."

"Good to know." Dominic had Augustin slung over a shoulder. Seconds later, he planted him on a worktable.

"I need some whisky." A groan left Augustin's mouth. "And lots of it."

Unsure of what I now saw—or if my eyes played tricks on me—I approached the table, gaze glued to the crimson coloration soaked into the leg of his jeans. "That's . . . wait, is that blood?"

"Yep. It's what happens when a prick-of-an-asshole takes a shot. Lucky for me, the fucker had a shitty aim." Augustin's rounded eyes held a deep-seated pain in them. "Fuck. Someone get me some whisky to numb this shit."

28

Salvador

"Ya got steady hands." Spider sat on a bench not far from the worktable where Dominic held Augustin down for Dr. Rafa to clean out a gunshot to the upper leg. "Cindy, right?"

"Yeah, that's my name. Thanks," she replied.

"Who taught you to stitch wounds?" Spider took a swig of bourbon.

"You did, five minutes ago when you told me to close it up." replied Cindy. Her laser focus remained on the second three-inch slice across Spider's arm, this one on his bicep.

My girl's full of surprises.

Watching her stitch someone up wasn't

anywhere near what I thought I'd see her doing today.

"What the fuck?" shouted Augustin. "You looking to touch bone? Fuck!"

"Be still and stop complaining." Rafa slid a metal instrument, *forceps, I think*, out of Augustin's thigh. He held the curved tip of the equipment at eye level. "Ahh, just as I thought." He then proceeded to utter a tsk, tsk, tsk.

"What's just as you thought, Doc?" asked Augustin.

"It's a solid." The doctor seemed rather pleased with himself. "Not a hollow-point, as I had first feared."

"What's he talking about, Sal?" Cindy's eyes bore into mine.

"Bullets," I replied. "Solid tips result in less meat or tissue destruction, usually."

"And hollow-points scatter projectiles," said Spider. "Resulting in more widespread damage."

The doc tapped Augustin on the shoulder with his elbow. "And there wasn't any ricochet. So, there's that too. Now, lay your lucky, scrawny ass on the table before I have the Russian and the Italian strap you down."

"Fuck you." Augustin's words slurred a bit. He extended a hand and shoved the doctor back a few steps. "Just do your job."

Filipe grabbed one of Augustin's arms, keeping him from toppling off the table.

"You're a tough little fucker. I'll give you that much." The Russian slammed Augustin to the table. "But you're also annoying as fuck when drunk. If you don't do what the doc says, I'm gonna do more than restrain you. I'm gonna knock you the fuck out."

"I'd like to see you try it." Augustin pulled his body up to a partial sitting position.

"Dude," I chimed in. "Just do what the doc says."

I'd never seen Augustin lose his shit like this. Well, maybe once or twice when Isa's life had come into play.

Thoughts of what Mina had said in the call prior came back, whispering in my head.

Fuck. Where did Juan Carlos and the Torres brothers get off to?

A glance in Mina's direction revealed the girl she'd brought back, one of Jorge's daughters.

Did they say he had two?

Blood stained the girl's clothing and Mina's as well.

Damn. Did something happen to the other one? To the other chica?

My thoughts turned back to Juan Carlos and the

Torres brothers, as well as the girl's father, Jorge. Dominic had stated they all ran, scattered during a double ambush.

A buzz hit my phone. At a quick glance, an alarm populated the screen. Someone had approached the front door of the club, and that someone was a thorn in my ass—a giant, prickly one at that.

"Fuck," I whispered the word under my breath.

Spider was the first to react. "What's up?"

"We got company outside," I replied

"Who?" asked Spider.

"A local cop, Rios." A heavy sigh left my lips.

I didn't have the patience to put up with this shit today.

I've reached my limit of the amount of fuckery I can handle for one day.

"He gonna be a problem?" asked Spider.

"Maybe." I pocketed my phone. "Hey, listen up," I called out.

All eyes in the room fell on me, and I do mean all eyes, including Mina and the *chica* under her care.

What is she, like, sixteen? The thought of what the Mad Dog and his men put her through, turned my stomach.

"Officer Rios is snooping around the front." I made my way to the opening of the hallway. "So, keep him quiet." I pointed at Augustin.

"I'm on it." Filipe pulled a silk handkerchief out of his pocket, then shoved it inside Augustin's mouth, then picked up a roll of duct tape off a counter.

"He's gonna kick your ass," said Marciano, who approached the worktable to secure Augustin's legs.

"Maybe if he remembers and only if he can catch me." Filipe winked at Marciano.

Stepping into the hallway, silence greeted me—a welcome changed from the events going on in the stockroom. About six feet in, the patter of light steps caught my ears, and I tossed a glance over a shoulder.

"What are you doing?" I asked.

"Coming with you," said Cindy. "As the manager on duty, I might be able to help."

A nod was the only response I gave her.

At the front door, I found Officer Rios and a handful of other officers waiting.

"What can I do for you, Officer?" I shouted through the glass window of the door. "We're not open yet."

Rios motioned for me to open up, then slapped a paper against the window.

"Is that a warrant?" Cindy leaned in closer.

"Maybe." I unlocked the door, then opened it.

Rios stood with a shit-eating grin. "Police—we're here to execute a search warrant!"

"May I see that?" Cindy stepped in front of me, cutting me off.

"Is Miss Costa on the premises?" asked Rios.

"I'm her acting manager for the club. And you are?" Cindy held her hand out, motioning for Officer Rios to take a step back, allowing her to step out. "Again. May I read it? As is my right under the Texas Code of Criminal Procedure, Chapter 18, Search Warrants."

"Officer Rios." The man's eyes narrowed, and his gaze took Cindy in from head to toe. "Who are you, again?"

"Cindy Stevens, club manager, which gives me the right to review the warrant on behalf of my employer, Miss Costa."

"Oh, I remember you now." Rios stood to full height. His gaze drifted to her bandaged thumb, then to her blouse. "What happen? Where'd the blood on your sleeve come from?"

The officer's gaze darted to me.

"Oh, this," she gave him a thumbs up sign, giving him a closer look at it. "Cut it on some plastic packaging during inventory this morning. It really bleed, too." A frown hit her lips. "Gosh, I hope it doesn't stain."

Her comment made my lips twitch into a slight

grin, then I schooled my face into an emotionless void once more.

"May I see some identification, Miss Stevens?" asked Officer Rios. "It is Miss, isn't it?"

"It is." She handed him her identification, then once more, she extended her hand. "The paperwork, please."

"Here you go." Rios handed over the document. He sidestepped, waved to his men, then he proceeded to walk past Cindy.

"Not so fast, Offer Rios." Cindy countered his steps, then held out an arm. "Under the provisions of the law, I'm entitled to review the warrant prior to you and your men conducting the search."

The transformation in Cindy happened so fast it was as if someone had flipped a switch. She went from club manager to speaking legal jargon with ease.

Rios froze in place and looked Cindy up and down once more, as if trying to figure her out. "Fine. Let me know if you have any questions."

Yeah, that's my girl. No one fucks with her.

29

Cindy

Several different statutory provisions existed for search warrants. Systematically, my brain ran through a handful of them, then set up a checklist of things to review:

—*Date of Issue

—*Scope of Warrant

—*Name of Subject(s)

—*Address

—*Names of Investigators

—*Issuing Court

—*Signature of Magistrate or Judge

—*Reasons Authorizing Entry

The wet signature, the magistrates physically

penned signature, identified this document as the original, which in itself didn't constitute a means to invalidate the warrant. However, a few other things listed, or not listed, piqued my interest.

"Thank you for providing the time for me to review the document, Officer Rios." I handed the document to him.

"Now," said Officer Rios, "If you'll step aside, Miss Stevens, we've got work to do."

"Afraid I can't do that, Officer." I stood inside the open doorway, blocking the entrance, with Salvador directly behind me.

"If you don't allow us to pass, Miss Stevens," Officer Rios put a hand on his taser, "you'll be interfering with a police matter."

"Officer Rios, I have no intention of 'interfering with a police matter,' as you incorrectly suggested." I held his steely gaze. "On the contrary, I'm upholding my rights, and the warrant you've attempted to serve is invade."

"Excuse me?" Officer Rios took a step back and glanced at the paperwork. "How so? It's signed by the magistrate."

"It has his wet signature, no doubt," I said. "But it's still invalided."

"On what grounds?" asked Officer Rios. The vein

on the side of his forehead raised, and his face reddened.

"Well, Officer Rios," I said. "For starters, and probably shouldn't have to tell you this, but it fails to set out the facts of the statutory requirements. On top of that, it also fails to make a full disclosure of the facts about the person, or persons, making the application for the property warrant." I offered him the sweetest smile I could muster. "Plus, the warrant has a predated date set for tomorrow, not today, rendering this document invalid for that reason alone."

"I'll be back tomorrow." The steely gaze and iron-clad expression on Officer Rios' face slipped a bit.

"I'm sure you will." I waved him off, then said, "Officer Rios. Might I offer a word of advice?"

"What would that be, Miss Stevens?"

"Ensure the document contains the correct physical address next time as well." I waved once more. "Oh, and Officer Rios . . ."

The officer turned to face me, along with a few of his men.

"Thank you for your service." A grin played on my lips. "It's men like you that keep our little communities safe."

Anger contorted the officer's facial features. His

face, now redder than a Red Delicious brand apple, looked as if it could produce steam.

"Bye now." I waved all the officers off this time, knowing full well one of them, if not more than one, would run my name as soon as seated in a patrol car.

Well, this should really piss my father off. Instead of the normal, stifling guilt that usually came over me, I felt elated. *Let him explain this to his partners.*

"What did I just witness?" Salvador's words floated to my ears.

"The execution of the law as laid out by the Texas Code of Criminal Procedures, under Chapter 18 of search warrants." A grin split my lips. "Gee, I guess my father was right about one thing."

"Yeah, what's that?" Salvador wrapped an arm around my waist, coaxing me toward the door.

"That my education would come in handy someday."

"Handy?" Salvador opened the door, then waited for me to enter. "Is that what you call what you just did? You handed the man his ass."

"I kind of did, didn't I?" A carefree giggle left my lips. "Gosh." I turned to face Salvador. "That really felt good."

"What felt good?" Mina came around the corner, a confused expression on her face. "And what happened to Officer Rios?"

"Miss Stevens here invalidated the warrant, then she sent Rios and the rest of his crew back where they came from." Salvador slid behind the bar. "She handed them—"

"I handed them their asses," I laughed. "And I was damn good at it, too. They'll think twice about trying to serve an invalid warrant." The thought of what I'd just done hit me. "I brought it—me, I did that. I stood my ground."

"That you did, *mi pequeña paloma.*" Salvador grabbed several shot glasses and a bottle of tequila. "This calls for a celebration."

"And from the sounds of things, a promotion," said Mina. "Hey, aren't you a law student? Isn't that what I read on your application?"

"Yes, Ma'am." I nodded. "Just waiting to pass my MCAP."

"Then this really is a celebration." Mina smiled. "Drinks on the house."

Salvador filled up several shot glasses.

"Hey," Filipe rounded the corner with Marciano on his heels. "What are we drinking to?"

"The woman of the hour." Mina picked up a shot glass. "My personal attorney, if she'll take the position."

I grabbed one of the drinks and brought it to my lips.

"Oh, Darling, you better believe your sweet ass that I'll drink to that." Filipe strutted to the counter.

"Me two." Marciano winked, then his gaze dropped to Filipe's backside. "Here's to promotions and sweet asses. May there be many, many more to come."

30

Salvador

"What do you think?" I stood in the opening between the bathroom and Filipe's bedroom.

"*Oh, qué lindo.*" The pure joy on Filipe's face had me wanting to knock the fuck out of him. "Don't you think he's cute?"

He pulled me into the middle of the room. "For fuck's sake."

Marciano walked around me as if taking in my clothing for the first time instead of the hundredth or thousandth time.

One would think he or Filipe were going to the gala instead of me.

How they got such a hard-on for dressing up in this stuffy-ass shit is beyond me.

"You said that to the last five things I tried on stuff, Filipe." The irritation in my voice clipped my words.

"Just look at him." A grin spread across Marciano's face. "*¡Qué chula!* Our little boy is growing up."

He pinched my cheek, and I smacked his hand away. "Dude, don't think I won't lay you out."

"*Touché. Touché.*" Marciano's face wore a scowl for about three seconds, then a frown hit his lips. "It's nice, but—"

"But what?" I wasn't sure I wanted to know.

"What are you thinking?" asked Filipe.

"I'm just not 100% sold." Marciano circled me once more. "Let's take it from the top." He clapped his hands. "Chop. Chop."

"Naw." I shook my head.

Fuck that! That shit wasn't gonna happen.

"We're done." My phone buzzed on the dresser, and I reached for it, but Marciano beat me to it.

"Oh, who's calling you? *Paloma*?" Marciano walked away with my phone. "Is it her?"

"Dude." I snapped my fingers, then motioned for him to hand it over. "My phone. Now."

"*Ciao*, is this *Paloma?*" He paused a moment. "Oh, yeah, he's here."

I ripped the phone out of his hand. "Sorry about that."

"Was that Marciano?" asked Cindy.

"Yeah, sorry." Heading for the hallway, I shot both Filipe and Marciano a 'don't fucking follow me' look. "Give me a moment."

I shut the door, leaving them both in Filipe's room.

"What's up?" I asked.

"About tonight, uhm . . ." The hesitation in her voice set me on alert.

"What about it?"

"You don't have to go if you don't want to," she said. "I mean, I don't want you to feel as if you have to. You're not under any obligation. So, I'd understand if you didn't want . . ."

Her rambling told me one thing: she was a bundle of nerves. Tonight was going to test her comfort limits, and I wasn't about to let her go alone. That'd be like sending her into a den of rabid dogs.

"One question."

"Okay. What?" Her voice sounded so high-strung.

"Actually two," I corrected. "What time do I pick you up? And where?"

"Oh, uhm, I'm at Mina's place." Her tone conveyed a smile. "The event starts at seven, so maybe six-thirty, since the gala's being held only a few blocks from here."

"Then I'll see you at six-thirty or before."

"Okay." A little squeal hit the end of the word. "Oh, wait, do you need the address?"

"Naw. I got it." I checked my watch. "See ya soon."

It was fifteen till six, which if I left now, I'd arrive a bit early.

Better early than late.

Duo footsteps drummed behind me.

"Look, *Mejo's* all grown up and looking so handsome." Filipe held his chest.

"Don't start." I headed for the front door. "Thanks for the lone of the threads."

"Like he said, any time, *Mejo*." Marciano winked, and like the dick he was, he said, "Don't do anything we wouldn't do. But if you do . . ." He tossed me a box of condoms.

"You're a dick." I glanced over my shoulder at both of them as they laughed their asses off.

"But you love us anyway," shouted Filipe.

"Whatever." I waved them off, then climbed inside my Jeep.

The drive to the hotel where Mina stayed didn't take long. I pulled into my usual spot, then took the service elevator to the top floor.

A couple of the men I'd assigned to guard her place stood at the entrance. They eyed me up and down, void of expression, then stepped aside, allowing me access without uttering a single word between them.

Once inside, I found Mina's Russian bulldog sitting on the couch in the makeshift living room.

"He's here," Dominic called out, then he motioned for me to sit. "You clean up good." Then a grin hit his lips. "Filipe?"

"Yeah, and his shadow."

"You talkin' about the Italian kid?" He rose, then poured himself a scotch.

"That'd be the one."

"Want one?" He offered a drink.

"Naw, man." I waved him off. "I'm good."

The girls rounded the corner, and both the Russian and I sprung to our feet.

The basic black dress Cindy wore hugged her body in all the right places, and the mere sight of her made my mouth water.

"Damn, boy," said Mina with a look of approval. "Lookin' good."

31

Cindy

"And who is this?" My mother gave Salvador the once over.

Even though a sourness coated my stomach, a pleasant smile touched my lips.

"Hello, Mother." I hugged her, then placed a kiss on both sides of her face.

A combination of her perfume and the wine on her breath filled my nose.

"This is Sal, my boyfriend." And there it was. I had tossed out the word, hoping to make it stick.

"Boyfriend?" She raised an eyebrow, then leaned next to my ear. "Or boy toy?" My mother laughed at her tasteless joke. "What of Keegan?" Her gaze drifted to the jerk.

"What about him?" I tightened my hold on Salvador's arm.

"Nice to meet you, Ma'am." Salvador took Mother's hand in his, then planted a kiss on the back of it. "I see where Cindy acquired her beauty from."

"Oh, stop." Mother ate up the compliment.

She looped her arm around his, leaving Salvador with not one, but two women hanging from his arms. If the action made him uncomfortable, he didn't show it.

"I think our table is other there." I pointed in the general direction.

A quick scan of the room revealed tonight's gathering had brought out many of Dallas' elite, from the mayor to local business owners. But one man remained unseen by my eyes.

"Have you seen your father?" Mother grabbed a wine glass off the tray of a passing waiter.

"You sure that's a good idea?" I rolled my eyes and did a slight head nod toward the drink she now held in her hand.

"Undoubtably so." Mother took a long swing, draining the glass. "Oh, loosen up, Sunshine," she scolded. "Or you'll end up sounding dreadfully boring like your father. Lord knows that man doesn't have a fun bone in his body." Leaning into Salvador, she whispered, "Not a single one. And I should know."

"Mother." I pleaded with my eyes for her to reign in her personality, along with her hands. "Please."

"Oh, come now, we both know what he's like." She felt up my date's arms. "My, you're muscular," she purred. "Do you work out?"

Salvador maintained a neutral expression, which I'd need to thank him for later.

Another waiter carrying a tray of fluted glasses passed by. This time, instead of wine, they held bubbly—champagne. Mother snagged one of those as well.

"I'll take one of those." I intercepted the drink in her hand inches from her mouth.

A grin spread her lips. "Since when did you start to drink?"

"Tonight, Mother. Tonight." To reinforce the comment, I took a long sip.

How bad can it be? She had guzzled down the same fluid earlier, as if chugging a water bottle.

The moment the fluid hit the back of my throat, a series of coughs hit, making my eyes water.

"You okay?" Salvador's stoic expression cracked, allowing a brief grin of amusement to surface.

"I think so." Somehow, I managed to get out the words out.

The irony of where I worked, in a bar, yet I couldn't drink down one little sip without choking, hadn't alluded me.

"Oh, look." Mother untangled her arm from Salvador's. "It's the mayor." She left a sloppy, wet kiss on the side of my face. "You have fun with your brown boy." Her whispered words barely hit my ears. A grin hit her face. "But not too much."

In a flash, she left, making a beeline for the mayor—well, as straight of a line as she could under the influence of alcohol.

I bet she's over the legal limit.

"I'm so sorry—sorry about her comment, about all of it. My mother's, well, you saw her." A frustrated sigh left my lips. "She's a walking PI waiting to happen."

"PI?" asked Salvador.

"Public intoxication," I said. "I'm sure she's over the legal limit of alcohol consumption."

"You think?" Salvador wrapped an arm around my waist. "Careful." He ushered me to the left of where he stood.

Seconds later, a silver serving cart rolled down the aisle.

"Thanks." I remained in his arms, relishing the sense of safety he provided.

"I need a word with you." My father's crisp words cut into my confidence.

"Hello, Father." I turned to face him.

"Now." His eyes bore in Salvador's direction. "Alone."

"Where I go"—I tightened my grip on Salvador—"he goes."

"And you are." My father didn't even bother to speak in a civil tone.

"Salvador Vargas," He extended a hand, and on reflex, my father took it. "I'm Cindy's boyfriend."

"Boyfriend? Is that so?" asked my father. "And what does your fiancé have to say about that?"

"Keegan Black isn't my betrothed—never will be."

"That's not what he thinks," said my father. "Nor what I've told people. He's practically part of the family."

I sucked in a breath, drawing strength from Salvador's presence. "If you're so keen on having him join the family, perhaps you should adopt Keegan. He could be the son you've always wanted."

32

Salvador

Puckered assholes lingered around the table for as far as the eye could see.

All around me, people rubbed elbows and kissed asses—two things I didn't fuckin' care for. But on the bright side, I had a beautiful woman next to me. One who wanted me for who I was, not because of my family relations, business opportunities, or the size of my bank account.

"You okay?" she asked softly, then squeezed my hand under the table.

"Yeah. You?" I caught sight of the slimy little fucker, Keegan.

How the fuck did he escape the River House?

On closer inspection, this carbon copy of him appeared younger.

"A younger clone?" I whispered, nodding toward the Keegan lookalike.

She leaned in next to me. "Younger brother."

If the kid had lasers for eyes, his fuckin' gaze would've burned a hole in the side of my head already.

Cindy laced her fingers with mine. The way her smaller palm perfectly fit inside of mine brought a grin to my lips.

"So, Cindy, does he speak?" asked her father. "Or is he only a display model?"

"He—" Her eyes widened, and she clutched my hand tighter.

"I speak." I shot her the politest 'I got this covered' glance I could conjure.

"What do you do?" asked her mother. "Sal, was it?"

"Yes," I replied.

"What does Sal stand for?" asked her father. The disdain burning in his eyes almost match that of Keegan Black's.

"Salvador." Once again, I kept my response short.

"And what do you do, Sal? What are you into?" Her mother downed half a glass of wine in one long drag.

"Security services." I stroked Cindy's hand with the pad of my thumb.

The air kicks on, blowing overhead. Goose bumps erupt across Cindy's arms. Without hesitation, I unbutton the suit jacket I'm wearing, slid it off, and then draped it over her shoulders.

"Well, now," crooned her mother. "Aren't you playing the part of a gentlemen?" She winked.

"That's because he is a gentlemen, Mother."

Mr. Steven's steely eyes, the same coloration as his daughter's, watched me with as much intent as a bird of prey stalking its next victim.

"So, when you said you work in security, what did that mean?" Mr. Stevens asked. "What's that look like?"

"Sal handle's security for Miss Costa's properties." Cindy took a small bite of the salmon on her plate.

"What kind of properties?" her father probed.

"Miss Costa owns The Alchemist and is scouting other business venture opportunities in the area."

"What kind of business ventures?" he asked.

"You'd have to ask her." I held the man's gaze.

"You're a man of few words, aren't you, Mr. Vargas?"

I remained silent, allowing him to draw whatever fuckin' conclusion he pulled out of thin air.

A waiter approached. He had a hand towel draped over one arm, and a fuckin' expensive ass looking bottle in the other.

"A sample, Sir?" asked the waiter.

Her father nodded, grasped the stem of the fluted glass, then smelled the contents.

"Sal," Mr. Stevens said. "Do you enjoy wine tasting? Have you ever been?"

"No." I shook my head once. "On both accounts."

"That's a shame," he said with a sigh. "Women are like fine wine. Some of them have a more expensive taste than others and just need to air out a bit before they come around. And they *always* come around. But, since this isn't your scene, you wouldn't know anything about that, would you?"

"Mr. Stevens," I cleared my throat. "I know all I need to."

"And what's that?" Mr. Stevens asked.

"A high-end bottle of wine and a cheap one results in the same outcome."

"Pray tell."

"The consumption of either one of them ends in inebriation," I said. "But we're not talking about wine here. No, we're talking about your daughter. A woman who could run circles around you and your partners. She's the new wave of the future, the next generation of law. And you and your ideas, they've already hit the rock bottom of the bottle."

The table had grown silent, and all eyes had fallen on Mr. Stevens.

His lack of respect for his wife—and more importantly for his daughter—annoyed the fuck out of me.

He fails to see the beauty, the brains behind his daughter—the woman I care about. The words rang true in my head. *I love her.*

The mental confession made me feel at ease with myself, with Cindy, and with the overall situation in general.

"The air has grown stale." I rose, then extended a hand to Cindy. "Shall we get some fresh air, *mi pequeña paloma?*"

"Yes. But of course." Cindy sat her napkin down, then placed her hand in mine. "That would be lovely. Thank you."

With a gentle tug, I pulled Cindy to her feet and into my arms. "It would be my pleasure."

"No, the pleasure is all mine." She placed a chaste kiss against my cheek, and my dick jerked to attention.

33

Cindy

"Hey, *Güera*." Filipe slid onto a barstool. "Aren't you going to the wedding?"

It was hard to imagine almost a week had passed since I had first climbed on the back of Salvador's motorcycle. But it had, and I couldn't be happier.

"*Güera?*" Drying a beer mug, I glanced over my shoulder. "What's that mean?"

"Means fair-haired, *Paloma*." Marciano took the seat next to Filipe. "Answer the question. You're going, yes?"

"Yeah." I nodded. "Sal's picking me up from here, then we'll head over."

"Please tell me that's not what you're wearing." Filipe waved his hand up and down with a dramatic flair only he could pull off.

"No, of course not. I have a dress hanging in the back."

"In Mina's office?" asked Filipe.

"Yeah, why?" I shelved the mug, then grabbed another out of the drainboard.

"Oh, I gotta see this." Filipe hopped off the barstool, then made his way to Mina's office.

Thoughts of his sewing kit came to mind, and I inwardly cringed.

"Please don't add any finishing touches, okay?" No response came my way. "Filipe, did you hear me?"

"Oh, *Paloma*." Chuckled Marciano. "You might want to see what he's doing." He winked.

After drying my hands, I hung the towel, then headed to Mina's office.

"Filipe," I called out. "What are you doing?"

"Oh, *Güera*," squealed Filipe. "Why didn't you tell me you were gonna wear an Infiwing dress—in royal blue, no less?"

Marciano entered Mina's office right after I did.

"Oh, *Bello*," crooned Marciano. "I bet this brings out your eyes, no?"

"Do you think it's too much? I want to make a good impression, but not over do it."

Now, I felt unsure of my selection.

"It's one of the few things that didn't get ruined in the break-in." A touch of sadness hit. "Should I just wear something else?"

In reality, I really didn't have anything else. It was this, the black dress I wore the other day, or what I worked in.

"Maybe I shouldn't go. I could call Sal and explain. He'd understand, right?"

"No." Felipe shook his head. "Go." He pointed at the attached bathroom. "Put it on. Now, *Meja*."

Still unsure, I took the dress from his hands, then headed to the bathroom.

"Without a bra, *Bello*," Marciano called out. "Set the girls free. You'll think me later."

"And so will Salvador," replied Filipe.

"I heard that, Filipe."

Snickering met my ears behind the closed door, but I couldn't tell if one or both of them now laughed.

Alone in the bathroom, I contemplated keeping my bra on or off. "But it's strapless."

"No, *Bello*," replied Marciano. "Don't make me come in there with Filipe's scissors."

The doorknob jiggled, making me jump.

Did I lock it?

My eye widened. I dashed to the door, then quickly twisted the lock. Behind the security of the door, I slipped out of my blouse and pants and glanced at my image in the mirror.

The red lacy panties I'd selected for the evening hugged my body with a butterfly scalloped lace. One thought came to mind.

I hope he likes them. A smile played on my lips.

Drawing in a deep breath and summoning all the confidence I could, I slipped out of my bra and into the dress.

The long straps of the top panels draped over my shoulders and hung down my back. Just as I had done last night when picking it up, I toyed with a few different ways to tie it. Finally, I decided on a simple design that provided a bit of a sleeve on my shoulders, crisscrossed the fabric panels in the back, then brought them to the front to tie.

"Are you done yet, *Bello*?" Marciano rapped on the door.

"Just about." I slipped on a pair of matching flats, then opened the door.

"Oh, *Güera*." Filipe smiled. "You have all kinds of curves you hide under your clothes."

Warmth hit my face, and from the intensity, I knew a visible blush had covered my face.

"Do you think it looks too much like a bridesmaid's dress?" A frown marred my lips. "It's what I wore to a family friend's wedding. It does, doesn't it?" I plopped on the couch. "I'm not going."

"Oh, you're going." Filipe took hold of my wrists and pulled me to my feet. "You wouldn't want to leave Salvador hangin', would ya? His *Tia*, well, to say that she's intense is an understatement. And *Meja*, she's expecting to meet you."

"How do you know that?"

"Because she told my Uncle Rafa," said Filipe. "Hell, she's been telling everyone that Salvador has a girl."

Butterflies swarmed in my stomach. *Is that what I am? What I want?*

"It's not like that," I replied.

"Yeah, keep tellin' yourself that, *Bello*." Chuckled Marciano. "I've seen the two of you together."

Filipe got to work on the top of the dress, by the time he finished, he had made the straps thin over my shoulders by twisting the fabric, crisscrossed the material over my back, then brought the panels to the front to give my bust some outline and finally tied them together at my lower back, allowing the excess fabric to hang loosely.

"What do you think?" Filipe stood me in front of a mirror.

"I'm not sure." I cupped my breasts. "I think I should put on my—"

"No," shouted Filipe.

"The girls need freedom," said Marciano. "Don't hide your assets more than you have to, *Bello*."

"Hmm." Filipe walked around me.

"What?" My heart thundered in my chest.

"One more thing," said Filipe. "Do you trust me?"

"Uhm." I thought hard about what he said, and in truth, I did. "Yes."

"Then close your eyes," he replied.

"Why?" I narrowed my eyelids, trying to figure out what he was up to.

"Because I have one last finishing touch."

"Fine." Eyes closed, I listened to the surrounding sounds.

He smoothed the fabric of the dress over my hips and legs. Then an oddly familiar noise sounded.

"Wait, a-are you cutting my dress?" My eyes flew open.

A gasp left my lips.

"I am," said Filipe. "You gotta trust me. Now, you'll look like the girlfriend instead of a bridesmaid."

Once he had finished cutting the bottom at a

symmetrical angle, I had to admit, it did look stylish. Plus, I liked the way the remaining fabric swished around my legs.

"Ah, *Bello*," said Marciano. "You look *magnifico*." He tossed a kiss in the air.

34

Salvador

"You look nice." I pressed the palm of my hand to the small of her back.

"It's not too much?" Her nervous gaze darted around the wedding venue.

"Not at all." I shook my head.

"Are you sure?" she asked. "During the wedding, people stared." She glanced around again. "And now, here at the reception, people are staring at me again."

"They're looking because you're beautiful, *mi pequeña paloma*. Nothing more."

"Come. Come." *Tia* Carmen grabbed one of my hands and one of Cindy's. "You both gotta play. Go."

She shooed both of us onto the open dance floor. "Don't make me tell you twice."

"What's going on?" asked Cindy. "What does she mean by play? Like a game?"

"Do you see the forming lines of people?"

"Yeah." She glanced around once more. "Why are we in a line?"

"To pass a balloon." I pointed to the other end of the line in front of us. "Like that."

She watched the first two people pass the balloon from one person's neck to the next.

"We're doing that?" Her eyes grew as wide as little pools of oceans.

"Yep." I nodded. "Looks that way." A grin spread my lips.

"What if I drop it?" Her anxiety had her wringing her hands together. "I don't want to be the reason the line loses."

"Relax." I drew her into my arms. "It's only a game—you know, for fun."

Her gaze bounced around the room, watching the other lines. No doubt, trying to get a handle on what the event entailed.

Each time someone dropped the balloon in a lineup, she or he walked to the back of the line with it, and the process started over once again. The person behind me, one of my cousins on my mother's side, Rita, I think, tapped me on the shoulder. She held the balloon, ready to pass it my way.

Seconds later, I had the balloon tucked between my chin and chest, and approached Cindy. I drew her into my arms and proceeded to pass the blue balloon. Mid-pass, it slipped out from between the two of us, hit the ground, then popped.

"Oh, gosh," Cindy turned a crimson color, and her eyes grew even larger than I thought possible. "I am so sorry, everyone. I didn't mean for it to—"

The men in the reception all hall stomped their feet, keeping a steady cadence. A few beats later, the women started clapping, and I knew what came next.

Mi pequeña paloma, you're in for a surprise. I chuckled to myself.

"What's so funny?" She glanced around the room.

People rose from the tables, and along with those still in line, converged, gathering around us.

"*Besar. Besar,*" the combined voices of the people in the reception hall chanted.

"What are they saying?" She swallowed hard.

I held her close, then whispered in her ear. "*Besar* means kiss."

Bowing my head, I pressed my lips to hers, claiming her mouth. Her body tensed.

A small gasp escaped her parted lips. I took the

opportunity to capitalize on the moment and plunged my tongue into her mouth, tasting her. After a few seconds, her body relaxed in my arms, and I deepened the kiss, knowing full well, my *Tia* Carmen would corner me or Cindy or both of us at some point to ask nosy questions. But at the moment, I couldn't care a less.

When I finally broke the kiss, it left her breathless and flushed, but this time for a whole other reason. The sexual attraction I felt for her had my dick harder than a fuckin' steel rod.

Fuck, if this keeps up, I'm gonna suffer from blue balls.

"Hey, don't stress out," I whispered in her ear, "but my *Tia* Carmen's on a collision course." My lips brushed against her neck, and she moaned, trembling in my arms.

"So, this is her? Really, her?" *Tia* Carmen approached. Her eyes narrowed on me. "And you didn't think enough of your Tia to introduce me? And what, you had the wedding, the reception, all this time . . ."

"Yes, *Tia,* it's really her. Meet my girl, Cindy Stevens." I wrapped an arm around her waist, drawing her closer to my frame.

"*Aye, Meja.*" My *Tia* wrapped her arms around

Cindy, lifting her off the ground in a bear hug. "It's finally good to meet you for real."

"Uhm, you too," replied Cindy. "Sal's told me so much about you. Him and his father." She looked around. "The wedding, your daughter's. It was simply beautiful."

"Oh, thank you, *Meja*." Tia patted Cindy's face. "*Aye. ¡Qué chula!*"

My *Tia* patted her face once more, then squeezed her ruddy cheeks.

A closer inspection of her face revealed faint dark circles forming around her eyes.

Seconds later, Cindy stifled a yawn. "Oh, sorry. Long day at work." She smiled.

Mi pequeña paloma's *tired.*

"You have to come visit." *Tia* pulled Cindy into a hug. "I'll make *chili rellenos* and *mole.* Two of Salvador's favorites."

"Carmen, don't hound the girl," said Mr. Vargas, Salvador's grandfather. "Or you might scare her off."

"I will not." My *Tia* shook a finger at my grandfather. "Take that back." She followed my grandfather across the dance floor.

"Come on," I whispered in her ear, then laced my fingers with hers. "Let's go, while the going is good."

35

Cindy

"Your family is nice." I glanced out the window, taking in the night sky.

"Wait, did you go to the same wedding I did?" He chuckled. "My family's all crazy."

"I'd take a sweet, crazy family any day of the week over mine."

Salvador reached over, grabbed my hand, brought it to his mouth, then kissed it.

"You're welcome to my family any time." He grinned.

"Thanks, I appreciate that." Laughter bubbled on my lips. "Hey, can we swing by my place? I'd like to change."

"Sure." He nodded. "Hey, don't be surprised if *Tia* Carmen tries to plan a pre-engagement party."

"But we just started dating."

"Well, she's intense like that."

Several minutes passed in a comfortable silence.

"Did you mean what you just said?" asked Salvador.

"About what?" I rubbed my neck, then stretched.

"About us dating?"

Is he upset? Did I say something wrong? What if he doesn't want to date me?

"I uhm." I chewed on my lower lip, unsure of what to say. "Is that something you want, that you're interested in pursuing?"

My palms grew sweaty, and my heart fluttered in my chest.

"What do you want?" he asked me point blank.

"Well, what do you want?"

Salvador pulled the Jeep into the drive.

"What I want is irrelevant." His gaze locked on mine. "Tell me what you want, what you need."

"I uhm . . ." As much as I wanted them to, the words just failed to come.

"Either you want to be with me, or you don't. It's as simple as that. So, which is it?"

"I want . . . I want to be w-with you, but only if that's something you want as well."

"*Mi pequeña paloma,* I've wanted you since I first set eyes on you."

"You did?"

"Yeah, I did." Salvador opened his door. "And I still do."

Without waiting, he exited the Jeep, then made his way around to my door, then opened it. Extending an arm, he offered me a hand.

The moment my hand touched his, butterflies took flight in my belly.

"Do you want to come inside?"

"I do." He helped me out of the car, then drew me into his arms for a quick kiss. "Let's go inside." His forehead pressed against mine. "I think your neighbors are hoping for a show, but I'm not into sharing."

"Neither am I." My shoes dangled from my hands.

"Good to know." Salvador scooped me up and carried me to the door.

Once inside, I dropped my shoes inside the entry, then tugged him down the hallway, toward my bedroom.

"You sure this is what you want?" asked Salvador. "That I'm what you want?"

"I am." My arms looped around his neck, and I kissed his lips.

Together, as one, we made it to the bed. Reaching

back, I fumbled with the square knot, holding the panels of the top of my dress in place.

Salvador placed his hands on my hips, then reached around. Methodically, he loosened the knot, then worked toward unwrapping me. The moment the dress panels fluttered to my sides, exposing my breasts, a groan escaped Salvador's lips.

"You're beautiful, *mi pequeña paloma.*"

He bowed his head, then gently took first my right breast into his mouth. He teased the pink bud until it stood at attention, begging for his touch, then he moved onto the other side. The warmth of his mouth incited goose bumps to erupt across my skin.

With a single tug of the garment, the dress slid down my hips, leaving me in nothing but the red, scallop panties.

"Mmm." He glanced at the lacy fabric. "I like these."

"I wore them for you, hoping you'd like them." The heat of embarrassment warmed my cheeks.

"In that case, I really like them."

He lifted me off my feet, and a yelp of surprise passed between my lips.

"I'm going to enjoy tasting you, touching you. Making you mine." He set me down, then started kissing his way up my legs.

The thought of being his and having him claim

me made my heart flutter faster. A heat spread out at the center of my core, making me ache for him.

His hands slid over my body. Once he reached my panties, he looped his fingers around the delicate fabric, then eased them off my hips and down my legs. Gently, he coaxed my thighs apart, then buried his head at the "y" of my legs.

A deep-seated ache built with every lick, flick, and nip he executed. The moment the tip of his tongue touched my clit, a moan escaped between my lips.

"That's it." His warm breath blew over my sensitive skin. "Come for me."

He continued his skilled caress, touching, licking, and sucking. A sweet burn erupted at my core, and I trembled in the thralls of sexual release.

"Sal, please." I ground my hips against him. "I want to feel you."

"Are you on anything?" asked Salvador. "Birth control."

"Monthly injections," I replied.

"Glove or not?" he asked. "I'm clean."

I thought for a moment. I'd never had unsheathed sex before, never cared to even try it until now. But if sex with Salvador was anything remotely like when he stimulated me orally, I was game.

"I've not tried . . . I've never done this without one, a condom that is." I chewed on my lower lip. "But I'd like to with you."

Slowly, he slid up my body and out of his pants. With one sturdy pull, he tugged his shirt off. Positioning himself between my legs, he rocked his body forward. The motion rubbed the head of his dick across my folds, and when he made contact with my clit, a moan left my lips.

"Do you like that?" He asked in a whisper.

"Mmm, I do."

Once more, he rocked his frame forward, causing friction between his body and mine.

He slipped a hand between my legs, through my wet folds, then plunged a digit inside me. Like clockwork, he thrust his finger in and out of my body.

"Please," I begged.

Salvador captured my moan in a heated kiss. He slid his shaft through my wet folds, rubbing the head against my clit. When I didn't think I could take any more, he thrusted his hips forward, plunging inside me a few inches.

My back arched, meeting him. And each time he thrusted his hips forward, he sunk an inch deeper, stretching me from the inside out.

A whimper left my lips, and I pulled him closer.

"You're tight," Salvador whispered. "Relax and let me in."

With one final push, he sank balls deep with a grunt. He held his body over me, motionless for several seconds, then he started a thrusting, keeping a steady rhythm.

Wrapping my legs around him helped me meet his demanding thrusts.

A sweet burning sensation began to grow at my core, making my clit throb.

"Please." I ground my hips, grinding my mound against him.

"Don't hold back." His eyes locked with mine. "Come for me, *mi pequeña paloma*."

His words were all I needed, and in a wave of pure bliss, I came, shouting his name. A few more thrusts, and he joined me. Both the head of his dick and his shaft pulsed, expelling his seed inside me. The warmth surprised me, and the skin-on-skin contact felt good.

"You okay, *mi pequeña paloma*?" He withdrew his partially firm shaft from my body, then drew me to his lean frame.

"I'm more than okay." A smile formed on my face.

I snuggled closer to his chest and breathed in the combined scent of our lovemaking. In Salvador's arms, I felt safe, and for the first time in my life, I had a sense of belonging.

"Hey, Sal."

"Yeah." He kissed my forehead.

"I just want you to know something," I whispered in his ear. "You. Make. Me. Happy."

To be continued . . .

SNEAK PEEK

SOUTH MAFIA WARS: CLEMENTE

From author Paige Price comes a mafia strangers-to-lovers romance about a mafia soldier and the girl who turns his world upside-down . . .

Stay Tuned for more information on Book 5 of the South Mafia Wars.

MINE TO HOLD

MAFIA BRIDE WARS

From author Paige Price comes a mafia strangers-to-lovers bully romance about a mafia underboss and his rebellious bride . . .

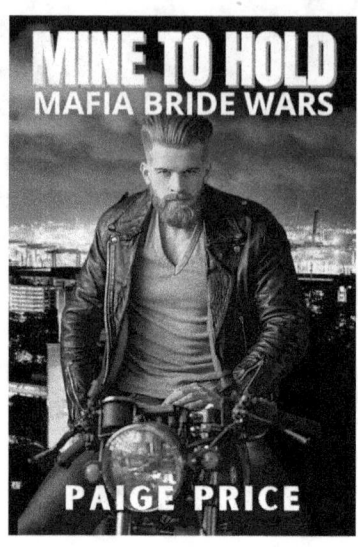

My hellish nightmare has a name, *Nicholas MacCarthy*.

He has one thing on his mind, strengthening the Brotherhood by any means possible.

Ardent
Arrogant
All-Consuming.

The man is domineering, high-handed, and over-bearing. He's about as warm and fuzzy as a scorpion ready to strike. He's ruthless, overbearing, and calculating. He's not above cracking the whip and handing out punishments as he sees fit. He's got another side though, one I both crave and view with fervent trepidation. But the man has ties to the Irish mafia, so I should keep my distance.

Angel Aisa-Biel is a hell spawn looking to claw her way out of the Mexican cartel as well as my bed.

She has the mouth of a sailor and seeks to spread her preverbal wings all in the name of freedom.

Defiant.
Disobedient.
Devilishly-Delectable

I have four rules, and my bride-to-be is dead-set on disobeying every single one of them.

Rule #1: No Running Away
Rule #2: Listen and Obey
Rule #3: No Talking Back
Rule #4: No Cursing

I'm not a patient, but I am a persistent man. A man on a direct mission from my *capo*: claim my bride. And I'll dismantle anything and anyone who comes between me and my future wife.

We share an undeniable connection and a common enemy that binds us together.

One look is all it took to capture my eye.
One fiery, heated kiss leads us to a red-hot passion.
One sensual touch sends us both spiraling out of control.

Claiming her as mine and ripping through her defenses is wrong, and I know it. But I don't care, not one bit, because the girl's mine to hold!

1

Angel Aisa-Biel

"Where the fuck are you, Angel?" My oldest brother, Alberto Jose Aisa, or "JR," as my family called him, screamed at me through the Airpods tucked snug in my ears. "Do you know what fuckin' time it is?"

Uh-huh. I can tell time, you motherfucker.

A grin stretched my lips, and a soft chuckle escaped my mouth. This morning, I'd found the tracker embedded in my phone, as well as the one in my car, and an hour ago, at precisely eight o'clock tonight, I had shut all that shit off.

I'm sure my father had everyone looking for me at this point, but I hadn't a fuck left to give. Graduation last week had freed me from his reign and, by association, his rules, not to mention all six of my brothers' suffocating shadows.

Well, at least, in my view.

Besides, it's not as if I needed my brothers, cartel soldiers, or any man breathing down my neck. And I sure as shit didn't need them telling me when to jump or how fucking high to go.

Hell no. I'm done with my father, my uncle, my brothers, and the cartel life in general.

A clean break, that's what I needed.

Starting the seventh lap of my jog on the St. Mary's track—the university I'd begin this coming fall—I disconnected the call without so much as a word, adjusted the baseball cap on my head, then picked up my pace, fueled by sheer adrenaline.

If I had a dick and balls between my legs, I wouldn't have to deal with this shit.

JR, the firstborn of my six older brothers, always had a stick up his ass. I couldn't wait to get away and live on campus. Only sixty-six days to go until my August move-in date, then maybe I'd be free of the testosterone-fueled *machismo* that had surrounded me my whole life.

Who am I kidding? Even now, that shit threatens to strangle me.

Another twelve laps and I had hit my target for the day—five miles.

Slowing to a shuffle, then a walk, my body began the cool-down lap process. A fourth of a mile later, I stopped at the bleachers and grabbed a partially frozen bottle of water.

The chilled fluid slid down my throat, washing away the dust from the track and the sour taste of my brother's words.

Overhead, a few stars made it through the city's light pollution and winked at me.

A shooting star streaked across the sky, and a smile danced on my lips.

My *Tia*, Eva Maria Navarro Aisa, once told me that wishing on a shooting star held more weight than blowing out birthday candles when I was six. And over the years, I had to admit, a higher percentage of my wishes done on stars came true in comparison to flickering candles embedded in a sugary, decaying frosted concoction.

Pressing my thumb to the touch-sensitive door lock of my Fiat, I waited for the audible click to sound, opened the door, slid behind the wheel, then put my phone in the dash holder. I was on the road in no time at all, making my way to my parents' estate.

An incoming call hit my phone, and I tapped the screen, sending JR to voicemail.

There's gonna be hell to pay when I get home. The thought made my stomach roll. *A hair over sixty days, and I'm a free woman—free of all this bullshit.*

Not having to answer to them daily was a change I full-heartedly welcomed with every fiber of my being. My older identical twin, Andrea "Ana" Aisa-Biel, didn't seem to mind the constant backseat driving by our brothers, uncle, father, and the men my father instructed to keep an eye on her.

Well, both of us. But I always gave those fuckers the slip.

Always her daddy's little *Princesa*! Andrea did everything the old man told her to do. Hell, she had even decided to take a year off from college because he suggested she do so, not me.

I can't get away from my father and his constant constraints and restrictions fast enough. Authority, I hate that shit more than anything.

My male family members' stifling attempts to control me had forced me to give all of them, along with the assigned muscle, the slip today, as well as every chance I got.

The engine purred to life, and I pulled out of the campus parking lot with a heavy sigh. Once on the main road, it didn't take long to merge onto the expressway before heading home. The further north of town I drove, the tighter my chest felt.

At the rate the traffic moved, I'd reach my final destination for the night by nine-thirty on the nose. If lucky, my father would be a drink or two away from shit-faced and would pass out on the sofa, in his office, or in bed.

Hell, if lucky, he'd drowned in the fucking heated pool he had to have.

My thoughts turned to the new life that awaited me on the St. Mary's campus in San Antonio. Sure, my fucking father had forced me to go to school in town, but the one great thing about attending an all-girl university—no men allowed, which included muscle as well. Plus, seeing his face a few weeks ago when I declared my major, forensic science, added icing to the cake of adulthood.

Watching him lose his shit had been a gift in itself.

I'd already packed all my stuff. I didn't mind living out of suitcases and bins for now. Hell, it wouldn't even take me long to move. Plus, it reminded my father that his days of keeping me under his fucking thumb were drawing to an end.

Petty, I know, but hey, I don't give a shit.

The Stone Oak Parkway exit came into view.

I eased onto the access road, then traveled the remaining seven minutes to the private entrance of the driveway. At the gate, I came to a stop, then rolled my window down to key in the code.

A shadow moved out of the darkness, making the shrubs shake.

"*¡Hijole! Meja.*" One of my father's trusted guards, more like his number three in command, Eric Valenzuela, stepped into view. "Do you know the shit-storm you've created?" He wore dark clothing and finished the ensemble with his third arm—a rifle strapped to his shoulder.

"Fuck, Eric." I jumped. "You nearly gave me a heart attack."

He stared me down for a few seconds, then keyed in the code.

"I'm gonna buy all of you shadow-walking-fuckers collars with bells on them, so I can hear every last one of you coming."

"Watch your mouth." Eric's usually stoic face held a tension I wasn't used to seeing.

"Whatever."

Tightlipped, he released a sigh that made his nostrils flare. "Go on. Get out of here. Your father's waiting."

"Yeah, well, that's nothing new."

"I wouldn't keep him waiting any longer, *Meja*. He's in a mood and has company."

When is he not in a fucking mood?

"Thanks for the tip." I sifted the car into drive, flipped him my left middle finger, then drove through the gate into the mini prison I'd called home for the last eighteen years, three months, and ten days.

2

Nicholas MacCarthy

"Sir, would you care for another scotch on the rocks?" The new flight attendant, Sally, Shelly, or Shelby—something beginning with an 'S' in it— fidgeted in the aisle of the Citation Longitude jet owned by the brotherhood.

If I had some free time on my hands and a riding crop or a flogger with me, I'd whisk her into the bathroom and teach her some self-control.

Hell, my hand sounded pretty good about now. My phone buzzed in the front pocket of my slacks.

"No. I'm good." I waved her off, retrieved my cell, hit talk, then held the device to my ear.

"You're late." I waited for Victor O'Sheehan, my number one man, to speak.

Using the trackpad of my laptop with my free hand, I scrolled through a spreadsheet, creating pivot tables to drill down into some offshore financial reports.

Late last night, my *capo di tutti capi*, Séamus Murray, the Irish mob boss of all bosses, none other than my Don, had called an impromptu meeting. All the *caporegime*—his captains—showed up at an undisclosed location in New York. So, I took the first flight out of San Antonio, Texas.

No one stands up a Don and lives to talk about it—no one. And as my father used to say, when the capofamiglia comes knocking, heed his call.

Additional meetings had delayed my return flight to San Antonio, Texas. So, I had sent Victor as my stand-in for a dinner engagement at Alberto Jose Aisa's home, the leader of the Mexican cartel, along with Isaac Doheny, my number two. A handful of loyal men had also dispatched to aid in the extraction of my prearranged bride-to-be, Andrea Aisa-Biel, from her family's estate.

Tides had changed. It was now time to claim my bride, whether she or her family liked it or not.

"Sorry for the delay, Boss, but there's been a

development." Victor O'Sheehan's voice finally hit the line.

"What kind?" Nothing I hated more in life than delays and unexpected developments, something Victor knew all too well.

"Seems not everyone felt the need to attend the mandatory dinner, Boss."

"Who?" Minimizing the spreadsheet, I opened the folder marked AJA on my desktop.

Thumbnail images of Alberto Jose Aisa, his wife, Valentina, and all eight of their children—seven sons and one daughter—came into view.

"Angel Aisa-Biel." Victor's voice came across the phone line.

I scanned the list of names, all starting with the fucking letter 'A,' and found an obscure image of a teen in a baseball cap and oversized sweats. "Andrea's twin brother, right?"

"That'd be the one. But I hear he's on his way now," said Victor. "There's more."

"Stop pussy-footing around." I didn't bother to hide my irritation.

"Your bride-to-be, Andrea, well, she isn't exactly the blushing bride her father had promised."

"So, she's not a virgin. Who gives a fuck?" Just about now, I was wishing I'd gotten that drink after all. "It doesn't change things."

"But I thought—"

"You thought wrong. Aisa got his fucking money, right?"

"Yeah," replied Victor.

"Well, he knew that when his daughter graduated, she'd belong to a member of our brotherhood—me. Now, it's time for him to pay up. The arrangement remains in place. So, you will return with my bride-to-be tonight, or don't return at all. Understand?"

"Yes, Sir."

Not a virgin. Fuck.

Initially, when told she was pure, the idea of breaking her in annoyed the fuck out of me. But over the last few weeks, the notion had grown on me. Well, along with the thought of plunging my dick into her tight virgin pussy.

"There's more." A heavy sigh hit the line.

"You better spit that shit out. All of it!" My voice rose a few octaves. "You feel me?"

"Yeah," said Victor. "Andrea's lover is a soldier for the cartel."

"Of course he is."

"He works for her father."

"Good, then one of you can kill that mother-fucker for taking what belonged to me."

The thought of having the asshole brought to one of my warehouses came to mind.

Fuck, I could torture the shit out of the thief. Teach him what it means to cross the brotherhood.

"Better yet," I pulled up Andrea's image and blew it up on the screen. "Bring me the fucker who deflowered her."

"Okay, Boss."

"When the last of the Aisa brothers arrive, message me. I want them to all know the deal's binding and that they can't do shit about it."

"Will do."

Victor disconnected the line, and I pocketed the phone.

The twin's absence left a bad taste in my mouth and had soured my mood. From what I could see, Aisa—the Mexican cartel leader—couldn't run shit, not even his family.

When a man lacks the respect and loyalty of his family, he's as good as dead.

Marrying into the family would put me in a position to take over the cartel endeavors her father ran. And from what I'd seen in the pivot tables earlier, some organization was in order.

"Hey, darlin'," I called out to the flight attendant. "I'll take that drink now."

"Yes, Sir." She rose from her seat. "Scotch on the rocks like before?"

"Yeah." I nodded. "Make it a double."

With my words, she took off down the aisle to the flight prep area. My gaze fell on the sway of her hips and that tight little ass of hers.

Hmm. Maybe there's time for a quick fuck in the bathroom, or better yet, she can wrap those pink lips around my dick for a while.

The thought amused me.

I could do with blowing off some steam.

3

Angel

The driveway was full, fuller than usual anyway, with vehicles I didn't recognize: three black SUVs and a dark F150 truck with an aluminum toolbox, all remained side-by-side. It didn't take a detective to know they all belonged to mafia members. No one called on my father that wasn't part of the so-called "business."

Hmm. Wonder what the driver keeps stored in that metal box: tools, guns, other weapons, or body parts.

The thought sent a chill to shoot across the length of my spine.

As soon as I pulled into an area to park, two men I didn't recognize approached the car—*gringos*, both of them. My brother Adreian Jose Aisa, the second born of the family, followed them.

"Where the fuck have you been?" Adreian opened my car door. One look at me had him sighing. "Seriously, Angel, you went for a fucking run?"

At the mention of my name, the *gringos'* eyes seemed to bulge out of their sockets, and then they took on the same emotionless, pasty-constipated expression as before.

"Yeah." I adjusted the baseball cap on my head, pulling my ponytail through the back. "I needed some alone time to clear my head."

"You could've done that here." His judgmental eyes bore through me. "I'd have gone with you."

"Which is why I jogged on campus." The words slipped past my filter, revealing where I had gone.

Fuck. Why did I tell him that?

The next time I slipped away, he and the muscle would check the track.

Of all my brothers, Adreian was the one who always coaxed shit out of me. Maybe it was because he had my mother's eyes—eyes that cut deep into a person's soul. One look at them was all it took to make me spill my sins like a sinner inside a confessional.

The *gringos*, one with red hair and the other a pale blond, kept staring at me as if they'd seen a fucking ghost. Their eyes kept drifting to my ponytail.

"What the fuck's up with them?" I whispered to Adreian.

"Well, if you'd been here for dinner and in your seat at eight when you were supposed to be, you'd know the answer to that. Now, wouldn't you?" Again, my brother's eyes judged me. "You should've been here for the announcement."

"Oh, fuck." A huff left my lips. "That was tonight?"

"Yeah," said Adreian. "And your seat at the table remained empty."

"Well, it's not as if my presence is ever needed." The way the *gringos* hovered around left an uneasy feeling in my gut.

One of the *gringos*, the one with a red beard, tapped his ear, and that's when I noticed both of those fuckers wore earpieces.

"No. No trouble at all. It seems Angel just arrived in *her* Fiat. So, it seems the family's all here now." The bearded man stared me down.

"What the fuck are you staring at, you ugly Ronald McDonald looking Irish fuck?" I wondered who the hell he had spoken to on the other end of the wireless connection.

A grin spread across the man's face. "Never seen a

Mexican with fiery hair before," said red beard. "How about you, Isaac?"

"Naw, never." Isaac shook his head. "Wasn't expecting a chick, either. Not dressed like that."

"Like what?" I fought the urge to roll my eyes.

"A guy." Isaac cracked a grin.

"Fuck you," I retorted.

I often wore Adreian's sweats or workout wear when exercising or when leaving the house because it kept people from bothering me. And I sure as shit didn't need to attract more assholes who thought they could wave their dicks around.

"Enough." Adreian grabbed my arm and tugged me forward. "Let's go. Dad's waiting."

"Don't touch me." I grappled free of my brother's hold, then hit his solar plex with just enough force to make him stagger backward and cough.

"Cut that karate shit out." Adreian rubbed his chest.

"It's time to go." That red-bearded motherfucker took a step into my personal space. The man was like a fucking refrigerator.

A loud boom went off, and Adreian dragged me to the ground. Seconds later, another shot fired, followed by a loud burst of automatic rounds. My gaze flicked to Isaac, then locked with the other Irishman.

Isaac was the first to make a move. "I'll secure the girl." He reached for me.

Out of instinct, I went into a defensive stance and blocked his approach. A commotion broke out next to me. My gaze flicked away from Isaac for a split second to take in Adreian and the other Irish prick brawling with fists.

Strong arms, the size of tree trunks, wrapped around my body and lifted me off the ground. Slamming my head back, I butted the fucker's face, and his groans of pain rewarded me.

"What the fuck?" Isaac loosened his hold. "You're nothing like your sister, are you?"

"No, not by a long shot, you fucker," I shouted. "Now, let go."

Twisting around, I grabbed his arm. Then, just as my sensei had taught me, I flipped him over. Just for good measure, I kicked him in the gut. The first blow hit solid, but the second, he blocked with his arms.

My focus then turned to my brother and the asshole who had him in a headlock.

"Run, Angel," shouted Adreian. "Get out of here."

"Not without you," I replied.

Closing the distance between my brother and me, I kneed the man on the side of the head several times. When he released my brother and stood, I swept his legs out from under him, sending him crashing to the ground.

"Fuck." Isaac groaned.

I grabbed Adreian's hand, then drew him to his feet. "My car. Now."

My brother's eyes widened. He shoved me sideways, and I stumbled a few steps, then hit the ground.

A boom cut through the night, and my brother fell to the ground.

"Adreian." I crawled on my hands and knees to him.

Blood seeped through the left side of his shirt, and he gasped for air.

"Oh, God." Tears stung my eyes. "What do I do?"

I pressed my hand over the wound, trying to stop the flow of blood, but it kept seeping through my fingers.

Several more booms sounded around me, but I couldn't tell where they'd originated from.

A strong arm wrapped around my body, ripping me away from my brother.

Screaming, I reached for Adreian, but couldn't get to him.

Muscle memory kicked in, and my body again went into self-defense mode. Grappling, I freed myself from the man's iron grip, then, with a well-placed kick to the side of his head and one to his groin, I brought the blond-headed, red-bearded Irish fucker to his knees.

"Adreian," I called to him, but I couldn't tell if he remained conscious or not.

A few steps away from my brother, and my body jolted forward.

My chest burned with a searing heat. Then every single one of my muscles tightened. They felt as if they would snap like an overextended rubber band.

Wire leads connected to steel prongs now protruded from my chest. Unable to control basic motor functions, I fell to the ground, convulsing.

"What the f-f-fuck?" My words came out light, airy, and breathless.

"You're a feisty one," said Isaac. "I'll give you that." He wiped blood off his face, smearing it into his blond hair.

"Not for long." The red-bearded Irishman with blonde hair pressed a knee against my chest, pinning me to the ground.

A glint of silver from a syringe flashed. The jab of the needle felt heavy, followed by a stinging sensation in my neck.

"What the fuck did you just give me?"

A shit-eating grin spread across the fuck-face's mouth. "Nighty, night, *Princesa*."

Still shaking from the effects of the taser, I struggled to regain control of my limbs. A haze clouded my vision. I glanced over at Adreian, who remained motionless on the ground.

"You motherfuckers," my tongue felt heavy, "I'm going to . . ."

Darkness, my old, long-lost friend, crept in, numbing both my body and brain.

This concludes the sample reading.
To continue reading this story, go to Amazon
"Mine To Hold" is the last book of . . .

Wicked & Ruthless: A Mafia Anthology

Want more South Mafia Wars?

ABOUT THE AUTHOR

Paige Price lives in Dallas, Texas with her husband, children, and four-legged family members. She found her love of writing, and her sanity, by developing a fictional dark mafia enemies to lovers' world during extended conference calls, hashing out love scenes on lunch breaks, and plotting her great escape from the corporate learning and development arena by creating the concept of South Mafia Wars, which she's excited to share with readers.